MOVE ME

EMMA
HOLLY

OTHER TITLES BY EMMA HOLLY

MOVE ME

Belle's eccentric Uncle Lucky left her his spooky house in the tiny village of Kingaken. Twenty years ago, her younger brother disappeared here, never to be heard from again. Returning to the place resurrects more ghosts than she cares to face. When it also summons a sexy faerie, with an agenda of his own, Belle prays her luck is better than her sibling's!

◆

Praise for the Hidden series

"A truly fantastic read! Ms. Holly turns the shape-shifting world on their respective ears! . . . 5 of 5 stars!"—**badasschicksthatbite.blogspot.com**

"I don't know how Emma Holly does it but I hope she keeps on doing it . . . a smoking HOT read and a great story."—**In My Humble Opinion**

"*Hidden Talents* is the perfect package of supes, romance, mystery and HEA!"
—paperbackdolls.com

CHAPTER 1

Belle Hobart, lately of Manhattan and all that was civilized, parked her rental car in the near-empty gravel lot beside Kingaken's General Store.

It was a bright fall day in the Catskills village: cerulean sky, turning leaves, postcard perfect in every way. The historic white clapboard house that served as the mercantile couldn't have been more picturesque. The film of dirt on its dark green shutters and the sagginess of its porch simply added to its patina. Though Belle hadn't been here in twenty years, she remembered both like it was yesterday.

Unease and weariness fought within her as she slammed the car door shut and tipped her two-hundred-dollar sunglasses on top of her straight brown hair. For good measure, she buttoned the smart tweed jacket she wore over her tastefully worn blue jeans.

Her feelings might not be as buttoned-up as she wanted, but she could damn well look as if they were.

The General Store's wood front steps creaked the same as ever when she climbed them in her vaguely equestrian-style boots. Inside, she found the usual mix of practical supplies for locals and tourist crap. Because the tourist crap was dusty, Belle concluded that segment of Kingaken's economy wasn't flourishing.

"Belle Hobart!" cried a woman's voice from the direction of the cash register.

The woman—plump, blonde, and as pretty as an apple blossom—hurried around the counter past aisles of soda and bread to pull Belle into a shockingly strong hug for such a small person.

Belle herself was tall and rangy, built on straight lines instead of curves. She'd been called attractive but never cute. Never girly. Never fragile. Never anything that seemed to inspire men to protectiveness. She had to lean down to pat her old school friend's shoulder blades.

"Hey, Susi," she said, feeling awkward as usual. "Looking good."

This caused Susi to push back from the embrace. "I look awful," she declared, her hand flying to her beautifully waved blonde hair. Her wedding ring's diamond glinted in the sun from the front windows, a slap of light in Belle's eye. "I'm a million years old and fat."

"Hardly. You're the same age as me, and you're still prettier."

Susi—*Gould* now, Belle believed—went blank with shock for a second before she burst out laughing. "Old Honest Belle. I forgot how blunt you could be. And how you never let people fish for compliments. I'm a whole year older, if you recall. Thirty-three now, Lord help me."

If she were a whole year older, she'd be thirty-four. Wisely, Belle let that slide.

"I heard you were coming back," Susi chattered on. "Sorry about your uncle, but it's nice the old freak left his place to you."

Belle's uncle Isaiah Luckes, aka "Uncle Lucky," had been an inventor and an

1

eccentric. He'd also become so reclusive that he was dead for six weeks before a curious postman tramped up his long dirt driveway to discover why his junk mail was piling up. The postman had peered through the ivy tangle on his front windows to find him peacefully decomposing in his favorite chair.

In case there'd been any doubt, Uncle Lucky's lawyer assured her he'd expired of natural causes. A fatal stroke was the ME's verdict.

Somewhat to her surprise, Mr. Tickner also informed her Uncle Lucky had bequeathed her his worldly goods. He'd never been warm and fuzzy when it came to family, but since leaving Kingaken with her parents, Belle hadn't received a single card or call from him.

"He did leave the place to me," Belle confirmed. "That's why I'm here. I figured you could recommend a local handyman. The lawyer warned me Uncle Lucky let the house run down. It needs work to be livable."

"So you *are* staying." Susi was bright-eyed at this bit of gossip she'd have to share.

"Don't know yet," Belle answered with a shrug. "If I decide to sell, it'll need work too."

"Well, I hope you stay," Susi said, seeming to mean it. "I'm sure Manhattan was exciting, but it can't have been home like Kingaken. People know you here. You've been missed."

Belle had been thirteen the night her parents shoved their belongings into a U-Haul and drove her "anywhere but here." She'd lived fewer years in Kingaken than she'd lived away from it. Nonetheless, she understood Susi's meaning. In small towns like this, where family roots ran deep, natives bonded to each other. Whether they liked you hardly mattered. They didn't relish seeing their own slip through their fingers.

Lord help me, Belle thought cynically, silently echoing Susi.

"Do you know any handymen who need work?" she asked.

"Don't I though!" Susi exclaimed, smoothing what was probably a hand-crocheted sweater down the front of her flowered dress. She was dressed exactly like her mother did in Belle's memories, down to her sensible flat shoes. "Come in the back while we're slow. I've got a couple numbers in my computer."

The mention of a computer reassured Belle time had progressed forward after all.

"How is your mother?" she asked Susi politely. She followed her childhood friend to the door of a small office. Inside, a cluttered metal desk claimed most of the real estate. The computer that sat on it was at least ten years old.

"Mom's good." A box of files sat on an old duct-taped rolling chair. Susi shoved both aside with her hip so she could lean over the keyboard. "She's still driving Dad crazy with her baking obsession."

"I got the recipes you sent when I was in college. That was nice of you."

Susi finished scribbling something on a post-it and straightened. She faced Belle with a sharp-eyed air of amusement. "Really? You thought that was nice? You never wrote back, you know. And you've no idea the amount of detective work I went through to track you down. Your mother hung up every time I called."

"Danny going missing was hard on my parents," Belle said, though her personal feelings about their responses were complicated. "After a while, they couldn't take the reminders."

Belle knew her eyes were dry, despite her diaphragm tightening. By contrast, Susi's pretty hazel gaze sheened over. She'd never stuffed her feelings down. "Danny was a sweet boy. People here still talk about him sometimes."

"It's probably the only place in the world they do." Belle's own words surprised her. She was playing with her jacket's single button, her hands twisting in a knot.

Susi reached out and patted her. "I think your Uncle Lucky blamed himself for what happened. I think it's why he turned into a shut-in."

Belle tended to agree. Guilt was also probably the reason he'd left his estate to her. Belle's mother had been Uncle Lucky's sister, but Belle's little brother was the only relative Isaiah seemed to like. Belle he'd tolerated because Danny adored her. With parents like theirs, whose own volatile emotions always seemed to matter most, she and Danny had found it easier to count on each other.

"It wasn't Uncle Lucky's fault," Belle said. "Nobody thought you had to watch kids that closely in Kingaken."

"And you never heard what happened to Danny?"

"Never. One minute he was playing in Uncle Lucky's yard, and the next he was gone."

"So he could still be . . . somewhere?"

"No," Belle said flatly enough to sound angry. She was done with hoping. She'd been done for a while.

Susi wasn't intimidated by her hard tone. She rested her curvy hips on the edge of the cluttered desk. "That private investigator you hired came around a few years back, asking folks questions."

"He found the same as the police. No leads. No clues. Not even suspicions."

It hadn't been tourist season when Danny disappeared. No one remembered seeing anyone out of place in town. If a stranger had grabbed her little brother, it had been on the fly. The weirder locals—among whom Uncle Lucky stood foremost—were all accounted for. In any case, none were weird in the way that led to abducting nine-year-olds. Belle's PI had ended up as stumped as the cops.

"Okay," Susi said placatingly, causing Belle to realize her teeth were grinding. "Look, honey, why don't I come around tonight and help you get settled? You don't need to be alone in that spooky wreck. I'll bring a bottle of wine and one of Mom's apple pies. You can tell me about the hot men you knew in New York."

Belle relaxed enough to smile. Susi had always been boy crazy. "That's nice of you. Maybe not tonight, though. I think I need to wander around on my own. Get my head sorted out."

"Soon then." Susi handed her the post-it. "That's my number on the top and John Feeney's on the bottom. He was laid off at the mill, and then his wife left with their three kids, so he's got time on his hands and a sparse bank account. He can do building, plumbing, and simple electric. He's a curmudgeon, but maybe you'll hit it off."

The wry slant of Susi's mouth said she thought Belle herself was one.

"Thank you," Belle said. "I want to catch up. I'm just not ready yet."

"This is Kingaken," Susi warned. "I sell the only groceries or toilet paper for thirty miles. If you're planning to avoid me, it'll take a fair piece of work."

Belle laughed in spite of herself. This was the Susi Jenkins she'd have been friends with even if she'd been born somewhere big enough to have a choice.

"Point taken," Belle conceded and bent to give Susi a quick hug.

For a moment before the feeling evaporated, she was glad to be home.

~

Belle's dread returned in force as she gassed the laboring rental car up Uncle Lucky's steep rutted drive. His house had to be half a mile from the access road—all of it uphill. Trees closed in on her from both sides: evergreens mostly, with a blood-bright scarlet maple bursting out here and there. The overgrowth turned her route into a gloomy tunnel, an impression that didn't lighten when she reached the equally overgrown two-hundred-year-old house.

Like the general store, the residence was two stories and white clapboard. Unlike the store, here the film of dirt had settled deeper—not so much picturesque as morose. Wildings, fallen branches, foot-high grass, and weeds lent the appropriate hermit's charm to the yard. Wisteria had swallowed the attic dormers, the flickering leaves making it easy to picture ghosts nearsightedly peeping out. The concrete birdbath where Belle and Danny had staged imaginary pirate battles lay in pieces by the barely discernible flagstone path.

Seeing the state the place had sunken into, Belle wondered why it had only taken six weeks for her uncle's corpse to be found.

She grabbed the groceries she'd bought at Susi's, then picked her way across the front yard jungle to the porch, glad for the protection of her tall riding boots. Scotch-taped to the chipped navy door was an envelope with a short message scrawled on it. Someone at the lawyer's office had let the movers in. The boxes of necessities she'd shipped ahead of her were inside. Nestled in the envelope was a simple metal ring with three keys. Belle pulled in a breath for courage and stuck the likeliest one in the lock.

To her relief, all she smelled inside was the recent cleaning someone had given the living room—not a cursory one either. Back in Manhattan, Belle owned a rent-a-maid service. She knew a good top-to-bottom job when she saw it. The wide plank floors were shining, the solid furniture covered in fresh white sheets. Though still shrouded in ivy, the windowpanes had been washed. Notably absent was her uncle's favorite leather armchair, the one he'd reportedly expired in.

"Thank you, Mr. Tickner," she murmured, making a mental note to tell the lawyer that in person.

Her stack of neatly labeled cartons sat in the center of the dark Turkish rug, but they'd wait to be unpacked. Belle intended to tour the house before her nerve ran out. Fortunately, the power and water hadn't been disconnected. The lights went on when she flicked the switches, and water ran from the tap. Very little had changed since the afterschool afternoons she and Danny had spent here, waiting for their parents to get off work. There was the farmhouse table where they'd done homework, here the squeaky screen door to the fateful back yard clearing. Uncle Lucky's library-office smelled precisely as she remembered, its shelves filled with musty books and odd natural specimens. He'd dreamed up his many inventions here: some lucrative, some completely pie-in-the-sky, but all more compelling to his attention than his niece and nephew.

Danny had been more curious than Belle about his activities. Her overtures had been swatted aside enough times for her to pretend disinterest. Because Danny was as smart as he was persistent, Uncle Lucky had thawed for him.

Magic is science, and science is magic, Belle heard him say in her memory. *Both seem mysterious until you study their principles.*

Most of Uncle Lucky's pie-in-the-sky inventions stemmed from his belief that the principles of both were valid.

On a nearby shelf, its spine sticking out slightly, a tattered black and white composition notebook caught Belle's eye. She pulled it out from beside the "nonfiction" *Goblins and their Habits* and opened it. Her heart clutched at the sight of the handwriting. This had been Danny's, written only months before his disappearance. He'd been nine, and Uncle Lucky had been teaching him what he called the language of the esoteric. Danny had learned it too. Belle couldn't understand half his childishly penciled words. *E pluribus Unum* was as much Latin as she knew.

Her throat choked up as her fingertips stroked the yellowed paper.

Danny, she thought. *I miss you.*

Though it caused her eyes to spill over, she kept the book clutched against her side for the rest of her wanderings. Upstairs to the three small bedrooms. Downstairs to re-light the pilot on the furnace. Everywhere she went, everything had been tidied. Uncle Lucky's clothes were in taped-up boxes, his personal items like toothbrushes and razors thrown away. The more she saw of what Mr. Tickner's staff had done, the more impressed she became. This was true thoughtfulness. She could sleep here tonight without feeling overwhelmed.

Small town people did have good qualities.

Heartened, she called the second number Susi had given her, before it was too late in the day to hope the man would come over. The shower in the single bathroom wasn't running, and—while she could take a bath—she felt more human after a pounding spray. Despite not being puny, a couple of the windows were jammed worse than her strength could open, and the rooms needed airing out. If no more than that was seen to, she'd consider the handyman's time well spent.

John Feeney picked up after the fourth ring.

He *sounded* like a curmudgeon, but Belle had been warned. Though she exerted what charm she'd learned from running her own business, he wouldn't promise to stop by that evening. He'd try, he said, but tomorrow suited him better. There was a game tonight, and he was settled in. To top off the sparkling impression he was making, his goodbye was as grumpy as his grudging acceptance of the job.

Belle snapped her cell phone shut with a snorting laugh. She debated calling Susi for another name, then decided to hell with it. She was on small-town time now. People hereabouts, no matter how short of funds, weren't necessarily going to jump for her.

Left to accomplish what she could herself, she cleaned up a little more, made herself a grilled cheese sandwich dinner, and—once she'd removed the sheets from the furniture—tried to watch her uncle's unexpectedly fancy dish TV. That service hadn't been turned back on, so she had a choice of browsing Uncle Lucky's creepy metaphysical book collection or finishing the mystery she'd loaded onto her too-small iPhone. As it happened, the mystery centered on a serial killer on a killing spree across rural America.

"Should have taken Susi up on the pie," she muttered.

Something rattled an upstairs window, probably the wind shaking the glass in its frame. Belle was used to the city, to the thick white noise of its million sounds blending. She'd forgotten how sounds stood out in the country.

You are not getting spooked, she ordered herself. Curmudgeons weren't afraid of bogeymen. Her hands gone icy, she pushed determinedly from the leather couch she'd sprawled on. Her ex-boyfriend Tom would have loved seeing her distressed. He'd always claimed she was too independent for her own good.

Bleh, she said to Tom's un-missed memory. Though he'd been cute and okay in bed, part of her had known she shouldn't depend on him. It was stupid to stick with people who couldn't take you as you came. Since, in the end, she couldn't take Tom as he came either, it was just as well they'd parted.

Susi's wedding diamond flashed in her mind again.

Because she didn't want to traipse down that God-you'll-die-a-spinster road, Belle forced her feet to climb the narrow staircase to the attic. This was the one section of the house she hadn't looked over, but if she was going to be haunted, she could at least choose the ghosts.

Fortunately, the bare bulbs that lit the attic were working. Beneath their sharp-edged glare, she found the sort of garret modern homes didn't have. Non-insulated eaves slanted to a cobwebbed peak, sheltering antique toys blanketed in dust and chests stuffed with lost treasures. Imaginative kids that they were, this had been Belle and Danny's favorite place in the house to play.

She suspected they were the last human beings to leave their footprints here.

She smiled through blurring eyes, which at the moment were watering more from the musty air than her nostalgia. Generations of Luckes and Benningtons had stashed their junk up here. Belle spied broken chairs and fringed silk lampshades. A cast iron kettle leaned in a corner next to a bicycle so antique its front wheel was bigger than its back. To her delight, her and Danny's prize steamer truck sat exactly where they'd left it in the center of the bare floorboards.

Hardly aware she'd moved, Belle dropped to her knees before it, undid the buckles, and pushed up the lid. The most extraordinary scent wafted out, not dust but a soft papery-perfume aroma—as if the past itself had been bottled up. Belle closed her eyes. With that smell surrounding her, she could see Danny's nine-year-old face: his ski slope nose with its splash of freckles, his straight brown bangs and bright green eyes. She heard his giggling laughter as if he were really there.

I'm the prime minister! he announced, the brim of a black top hat slipping down his face. *I'm marching to Parliament.*

He'd assumed a ridiculous British accent, much better at Latin than he was at mimicry.

I'm a flapper, Belle had returned, her skinny thirteen-year-old body swimming in its own outfit. *I'm going to swill Prohibition gin.*

When she opened her eyes, the costume from her memory lay on top of the trunk's otherwise jumbled pile. She'd folded the delicate garment, her characteristic neatness manifesting even at that age. The feathered rhinestone clips still attached the straps to the low-cut bodice. She could have smoothed them into those curls yesterday.

Unable to resist, she lifted the vintage dress and rose to her feet to shake out the dust. Gosh, the thing was pretty. Rayon hadn't existed when it was sewn. Real silk-satin caressed her fingers, stirring a sensual pleasure she hadn't felt in ages. The slippery fabric was midnight black, cut on the bias so it would cling. Her great-whatever relative's dress might actually fit her now. If it did, maybe in a couple days she'd convince Susi to join her for a night out in the next bigger town.

No matter how impulsive she was feeling, the attic was too dirty to undress in. Belle carried her find to the door. As she did, her path took her past the rear dormers. An eerie glow stopped her in her tracks. She stepped into the window embrasure to get a better look.

The light came from Uncle Lucky's old work shed. No garden tools were stored there. The ramshackle wooden building was where Uncle Lucky had built and tested his more exotic inventions. He'd abandoned it after Danny disappeared, going so far as to nail the door shut under multiple two by fours.

*I'm **not** spooked*, Belle insisted, her heart hammering in her chest. Maybe John Feeney had come over. Maybe the boards had fallen off and he'd lit a lantern to search for a spare hammer.

The problem with this theory was that the glow wasn't issuing from inside the shack's windows. It surrounded the whole structure, as if the weathered wood were infused with blue-white phosphor.

Belle, she thought she heard a voice whisper. *Belle, I'm so sorry*. An instant later, the light winked out.

Belle shivered so hard her teeth clacked together.

Whoever that raspy whisper belonged to, it hadn't been Danny.

CHAPTER 2

Dubhghall the faerie prince was in dire need of a new name. His truename (which wasn't Dubhghall) had been unearthed by his enemy, who could now use it to compel him against his will.

This would have been unfortunate in itself, but Mor was trying to leverage his stolen knowledge to extort the throne of Talfryn from Dubhghall's folks. Since Talfryn was one of the few stable territories left in Faerie, this fell under the umbrella of a Bad Thing.

Mor's own country had long since fallen into magical anarchy, which happened when an area's governors couldn't agree on what the laws of reality ought to be. Hungry for new land to rule—which he seemed unlikely to do a better job of than before—Mor pursued Dubhghall across Faerie, trying desperately to get close enough to spell him.

Mor was no tissue-paper foe. Older than Dubhghall's parents by half a millennium, he outmatched Talfryn's youngest prince. For a while, Dubhghall sheltered with relatives in the Pocket city of Resurrection in New York. That city's merely half-magic nature made it easier to hide from seeking charms. Finally, however, Mor tracked Dubhghall there. They fought an epic battle in the men's department of the downtown Macy's, injuring a number of less powerful bystanders in the fray.

Mor had the advantage of not giving a tinker's damn about them.

Though not as experienced or ruthless as his adversary, Dubhghall still knew a few tricks. He'd magically sealed Mor's mouth before the sorcerer faerie could use his Name. Enraged, Mor had stabbed Dubhghall in the side with an iron knife. Dubhghall repaid the favor by breaking a metal garment pole on Mor's skull. He'd escaped while Mor staggered, but only just.

Because it was only just, he'd known he needed to flee the magical world altogether. Dubhghall had been called spoiled a time or two in his life, but his parents had raised him to care about their people. For their part, they adored all their children to a degree almost unknown in Faerie. They'd hold out against the blackmail as long as they thought Dubhghall could. If Mor caught their son, however, if it looked like their baby would be compelled to magically attack his own loved ones, the king and queen might cave. Only among mundanes would Dubhghall—and Talfryn—be safe from Mor's terrible tactics.

As he sped across Resurrection's Catkin Park in the dark, the glimmering remnant of a portal caused him to lose his footing and go sprawling. He cursed at first, then realized his faerie luck was trying to help. Though not ancient, Dubhghall *was* a prince. Even depleted from the battle, he possessed sufficient magic to prize the interdimensional door open. He might not know where he'd land, but that very uncertainty would prevent Mor from tracking him.

Almost before he could think about it, he flung up his hand and chanted the appropriate words in the old language.

Light burst around the portal a second before it sucked him in.

He was Somewhere Else then, somewhere dark and musty and hard underneath his butt.

"Crap," he said, but not without a tinge of relief. The portal had closed behind him, saving him the trouble, most likely because its power was close to played out. Wherever he'd fetched up, he was safe for the time being.

He suspected he'd made it to the mundane world. His limbs felt sluggish as he pushed cautiously to his feet, as if the planet's gravity had increased. He pressed a hand to his ribs, where the scar from his partially healed knife wound didn't want to stretch. He sensed many trees close by, a woods perhaps. Neither their energy nor that of the earth came to him when he pulled, which meant his scar would be staying where it was for now. Normally, he didn't have to think about drawing up healing power. A faerie's reservoir of magic automatically renewed itself. Recharging their batteries was no harder for the fae than breathing was for others. Faeries embodied magic in a very literal way.

To be cut off from that for the first time in his long life was disconcerting, to say the least.

You hoped you'd land here, he reminded himself. *Don't start complaining now.*

He'd simply have to be careful not to exhaust his supply. And there must be *some* magic here. He knew from his stay in Resurrection that humans with Talent existed outside its borders.

His eyes began to adjust to the darkness. He stood in what looked like an abandoned alchemist's laboratory, though it didn't seem to have been used to make gold. Old chalk scratchings formed a circle around his feet, glowing faintly as the reactivated portal finished shutting down. Dubhghall stepped over the marks carefully. The runes weren't what he was used to, and he felt safer not smudging them. In time, he might try going home again, especially if he got what he needed from the mundanes.

The single door to the alchemist's shed didn't want to open for him. Gently, so as not to make too much noise, he pushed against it with his shoulder. The boards that sealed it yielded at the steady pressure, nails sliding out of wood as he heaved. Luckily, they were steel nails. Pure iron would have taken more of his strength to budge. Satisfied his good fortune was holding, he stepped into a crisp autumn night.

He found himself in a weedy clearing behind a human style farmhouse. The residence rose two stories, and all of its lights were on.

"Tell her I'm sorry," said a whispery voice.

Dubhghall spun toward the sound, his hands raised to defend himself with what magic remained to him. Fortunately, none was required to counter this threat. Dubhghall was being importuned by a ghost.

The shade—which had taken the form of a sad old man in a cardigan—was considerably weaker than the spirits he was used to. Dubhghall doubted it was up to stirring breezes, much less harming him. Slowly, he dropped his hands.

"Tell who you're sorry?" he asked.

"Belle," sighed the specter, the name mournful. "She won't listen to me."

If she was a mundane, she probably couldn't hear.

"Who are you to her?" Dubhghall asked.

"Her uncle." The specter flickered and came back, a candle flame guttering. "I left her all my earthly possessions, but she's still sad."

A prickle of an idea stood the hairs up on Dubhghall's nape. His luck might have led him better than he knew when it tripped him over that interdimensional threshold. "*All* your earthly possessions? You worded it like that in your will?"

The ghost nodded, then tugged its gray shaggy hair with transparent hands. "I thought she'd like that. Why is she still weeping in my house?"

Dubhghall shot a glance up at the lit windows. Mundane world or no, he sensed a living being within the walls. A moment's homesickness sent a pang through his heart. He'd been away from his family for a long time. When he returned his attention to the ghost, the lines of its face had pulled down like a Tragedy mask. Shades' emotions tended to be simple.

What wasn't simple was the fae's ability to strike deals that benefitted them. Their kind had rules against outright lying, the penalties for which were uncomfortable. Trickery, on the other hand, was considered a high art.

"Perhaps I could help Belle find happiness," Dubhghall suggested.

"Oh, could you?" the specter pleaded, its hands wrung together before its breast.

"Quite possibly," Dubhghall confirmed. "Assuming you tell me everything you know about your niece's situation. I'll need information to accomplish what you wish."

The ghost pulled its shoulders straighter, its pride apparent. "I've been listening," it boasted. "Ever since Belle came back."

"I bet you have," Dubhghall said.

~

Belle took twenty minutes to convince herself she was overstressed and imagining things. The shed was in the Back Yard, the same back yard where her little brother Danny had disappeared. Maybe its roof was wet and the light from the house's windows created the impression that it was glowing.

Avoiding looking at it again, she ate two Oreos to calm her nerves, a practice she disapproved of but indulged in occasionally anyway. Steadier but in need of diversion, she returned to the upstairs bedroom she'd decided to sleep in. Though Uncle Lucky's room had been cleaned, staying there was out of the question. In her chosen room for the night, she wriggled into the vintage dress she'd rescued from the attic. It certainly fit her different now. Belle didn't think she'd ever looked so siren-like. She stood in front of the freestanding mirror, adjusting the feathered straps, when the downstairs doorknocker rapped out a sharp rhythm.

The fact that she jumped a foot said she wasn't so calm really.

Chances were, her visitor was Susi. When they'd been kids, Belle's best friend hadn't been good at hearing *no*. Belle rolled her eyes at her reflection in the clingy plunge-cut dress. If she'd had an inch more up top, her cleavage would have been outrageous. Because she was relatively flat, she only looked overdressed. She wondered if she could convince Susi she always primped for pie eating.

In case Susi wasn't her caller, she grabbed the Louisville Slugger her uncle kept in the hall closet. Thankfully, Mr. Tickner's staff hadn't cleared out the bat.

"Coming!" she said as the knocker dropped again.

Holding her weapon slightly behind her, Belle opened the front door.

Every thought she'd *ever* had flew out of her head.

The stranger who stood on her porch was well over six feet tall. His hair and eyes were dark, his shoulders as broad as a quarterback's. He'd tucked the well-washed cotton of a plaid flannel shirt into loden green work pants. Though his trousers weren't snug, she could tell the legs that filled them were fit. A battered leather tool belt hung low on narrow hips. His large feet were clad in work boots with different colors of paint on them. A sheer but noticeable stubble darkened his jaw.

All these observations, though they sprang from within Belle's own head, might as well have been in Latin.

Oh. My. God, said a deeper and less rational part of her. This man was too delectable to be real. Her mouth was literally watering at the sight of him. She wanted to plant a kiss on his shapely lips—or maybe lick him all over. The zipper that curved gently around his package seemed a good place to start. Lower portions of her body grew wet at that idea. He was perfect without being perfect at all. His nose was a little long, and some might have objected to the ungroomed shagginess of his brows. His beard shadow made him look rough and masculine. He had weary circles under his eyes.

Belle wanted to kiss them too.

"Uh," was all her brain *or* her instincts agreed to let her say.

"I believe you're expecting a handyman," said her visitor, hooking long thumbs into his tool belt. He looked oddly like he was posing, but Belle wasn't inclined to complain. His graceful fingers framed his crotch perfectly.

"Oh," she said, scarcely an improvement on *uh*. She shook herself and swallowed. "You must be John Feeney. You came tonight after all."

"I did. Do you have things for me to fix?" He was looking straight in her eyes. Most men wouldn't have, given how she was dressed. Then again, considering his killer looks, women in skimpy outfits might greet him every day. For all she knew, John Feeney was Kingaken's most popular lonely housewife fantasy. He lifted the metal box he carried by the handle, no doubt showing off more handyman credentials.

Belle realized she'd failed to answer him for too long.

"Uh, yes," she said, stepping backward into the entryway. "Please come in. There's—" He'd moved past her, and her gaze zeroed in on the tight movement of his ass in the dark green pants. *Jesus*, she swore to herself. "There are a couple upstairs windows that need unsticking and a showerhead that won't spurt water."

Spurt was a stupid word, wasn't it? Probably she shouldn't have used it, if only because it made her think about erections and wrapping them in her hand. Did John Feeney have a long cock? His feet and his thumbs were big. That was supposed to mean something.

"I'm Belle Hobart," she blurted.

John Feeney paused with his paint-spattered boot on the first stair tread. Her cheeks blazed fire when he raised his dramatic eyebrows at her.

"I know," he answered. "You said your name on the phone."

His manners sucked as bad as when they'd spoken earlier. Annoyance helped clear her head. She propped the baseball bat against the closet door, then followed John to the second floor.

As she did, her heart barely stumbled around in her chest at all.

~

Dubhghall's first stop after speaking to the ghost had been John Feeney's house. The "handyman," a term he'd learned from watching the Import Channel in Resurrection, had been drinking cheap canned beer in front of his TV. With the man's resistance to enchantment lowered by alcohol, charming everything Dubhghall needed from him had been a snap.

As long as he was there, he'd flipped through John Feeney's collection of "How-To" books. Feeney had taken up his home repair business recently. If a human could pull this off, Dubhghall saw no reason why a faerie shouldn't. Not only was his race considerably smarter, they were excellent actors. He had no doubt his impersonation would hold up.

He left Feeney with a magical compulsion to avoid Belle Hobart and her job requests from now on. The expenditure from his reservoir was worth it. The fewer complications he had to deal with, the sooner he'd be out of here. Thus far, the mundane world wasn't enthralling him.

Despite the ease of his entrance, meeting Belle Hobart disturbed him. He'd been expecting someone red-eyed and miserable, a poor unhappy rabbit of a human. What he'd gotten was quite different.

Isaiah's niece was proud and beautiful.

Faeries had a long history of being attracted to humans. The stability of mortal lives seemed exotic: that each day would unfold along similar lines as the one before. Human emotions were warmer than the fae's, a contrast that acted like catnip on strong sex drives. Humans enjoyed making love with his kind, and that appealed as well, because who wouldn't want to feel like a god in bed? Add in the lure of the forbidden, and Belle's race was hard to resist. Fae and human couplings could produce children—a giant no-no for a people who valued pure bloodlines.

Too bad for him Belle Hobart had the demeanor of one of his world's queens.

Immediately, he abandoned his plan to get close to her by playing on her sympathy. This gorgeous woman in her insanely sexy frock wasn't anyone's hand patter. He wished he hadn't borrowed John Feeney's worn work costume. Being underdressed compared to his quarry put him at the sort of disadvantage he'd rarely experienced.

The skin along his back felt unnaturally hot as she followed him up the stairs.

"It's the windows in my uncle's room that are stuck," she said as they reached the second-floor landing. "I'd like to air it out in there."

Since her uncle's room was among the areas he wished to see, Dubhghall nodded. Apparently nervous, Belle smoothed the tail of chestnut hair that spilled in front of her left shoulder. The sheaf was thick and shiny, as straight as if it were spelled. Its ends hung lower than her slight breasts, drawing attention to the press of her sharpened nipples on the skimpy black bodice.

Dubhghall's temperature rose a few more degrees.

Possibly, Belle noticed him staring. Releasing her hair, she hitched her thumb toward the room behind her. When she spoke, her voice was thready from lack of air. "I'll just change into something more practical."

If he hadn't been pretending to be irascible John Feeney, he'd have told her not to bother on his account. But she was blushing sufficiently without him turning on the charm. Unnerved by his continued silence, she spun jerkily around, stalked into the room she'd indicated, and shut the door crisply behind her.

Dubhghall smiled to himself. No man could mind flustering a woman that lovely.

Freed from her observation, he stepped into the largest of the three bedrooms, presuming this to be the dead uncle's. Silently and swiftly, he opened and closed bureau drawers, knowing he might not have long to search until Belle returned. To his dismay, the drawers were empty. Finally, at the back of the highest shelf in the closet, he found a lidded box. Inside was a pale blue baby book belonging to the recently almost-departed Isaiah Bennington-Luckes.

Dubhghall turned the pages quickly, taking mental snapshots of the photos and captions as he went. Isaiah hadn't had as many nicknames as were ideal (perhaps he hadn't been an endearing child?) but he'd had enough to serve. The extra last name was a windfall, as was his middle name of Lewis. Best of all, in a special pocket at the end of the padded book, Dubhghall found a little envelope containing one curled lock of Isaiah's baby hair.

In a twinkling, the envelope and the lock disappeared into Dubhghall's breast pocket. Baby hair was golden for doing spells. No faerie mother would dream of leaving it around. Faerie mothers kept what keepsakes they wished from their children hidden in containers like magic walnut shells. Humans guarded nothing, for which Dubhghall was thankful. His future escape had just gotten easier.

All this he accomplished in under five minutes. By the time Belle returned, wearing what he'd learned were "sweats" in Resurrection, he was separating the stuck paint on Isaiah's windows with a box cutter. Firmly banging the frame with the side of his fists resulted in a pair of sashes that slid smoothly up and down.

Dubhghall enjoyed a flush of satisfaction. He'd solved Belle's first challenge without magic. Hercules himself could not have claimed more.

"Well," she said. "That was quick. Want to take a look at the shower?"

A manly grunt seemed the best response.

She preceded him to the bathroom, where a white plastic shower curtain surrounded a claw foot tub. Belle spared him some confusion by turning the taps herself, to demonstrate the shower's faulty functioning.

"The holes might be blocked by mineral salts," she said. "I have something I think will clean it, but I don't know how to take the showerhead off."

"Ayuh," Dubhghall said, one finger scratching his bristly cheek. He set his toolbox on the old-fashioned penny tile. He was feeling strange in the close quarters, too aware of the human female's body heat next to him. The increased heaviness of his groin warned him he was getting an erection. Belle wore the baggy gray outfit now, but that didn't seem to matter. She smelled nice, and her eyes were the murky green of a churning river, her cheeks and lips rosy from the blood rising into them. His erection strengthened, and he registered his own scent rising.

Letting that happen wasn't a good idea.

His kind produced a substance other races called faerie dust. Similar to a flower and its bee-attracting pollen, the essence lured useful beings to them. As was the case for bees, humans could get drunk on it, not coincidentally lowering their barriers to spell craft. To cap the matter, ephor was a mild aphrodisiac. The fact that he smelled the spicy-sweetness suggested it wasn't inert in the mundane world.

If he wasn't careful, he'd start sparkling.

Of course, being careful probably didn't include locking eyes with Belle Hobart.

His stare was affecting her. Her cheeks flushed a deeper red, her full lips parting for quickened breaths. Her response kicked off a vicious cycle. The more aroused she grew, the stiffer his prick became, until it pressed his zipper hard enough to hurt.

"Gosh, you smell good," she burst out.

He grabbed her face in both hands and kissed her.

Pleasure exploded in his mouth and palms. How long had it been since he'd kissed a woman? Not since he'd started running from Mor a year ago, he thought. With no reason to keep up his guard here, he shoved Belle into the wall beside the doorway. His customary coordination must have been shot. Her shoulder inadvertently knocked the light switch off.

That was fine. Darkness heightened the senses. He felt her writhing under him all the better, heard the broken moans that caught in her throat. The arms she wrapped around him were tight and strong, her body deliciously springy under his. Dubhghall pushed her long legs wider with one thigh, driving his tongue into her warm mouth. The eagerness with which she sucked him back made his scalp tingle. He rolled his hips more firmly to her, groaning at the pressure of her softness against his aching cock.

Sudden, her baggy sweatpants seemed like a blessing.

She moaned as he kissed a trail down her long smooth neck. He nuzzled the pulse that raced at its base, momentarily envious of vampires. Unable to take her in that way, he slid his hands to her bottom, where she had more flesh than at her bosom. Dubhghall squeezed her butt with relish, growling in approval at the way her curves gave.

Belle must have liked that too. The scent of female arousal spiked higher than faerie dust.

"God," she gasped, her hips rocking hard to his.

Dubhghall sucked in his breath at the jolt of sensation that spread outward from his crotch. He shifted his hands to slide under the soft sweatpants.

Belle stiffened like a board.

"No," she said, shoving at his chest. "You shouldn't—We shouldn't be doing this."

Dubhghall's lust-addled mind took a moment to get the message, but he let go of her. His knees weren't as steady as they should have been; it *had* only been a kiss. He took comfort in the fact that Belle was breathing unevenly when she flipped the light switch back on.

"Look," she said. "I know your wife running off on you was crappy, but you can't just jump into this with me."

"I'm not married," he said firmly, which was the honest truth.

"So you're recently divorced and rebounding. I broke up with someone not long ago. I know a person's judgment isn't the greatest right after that."

Despite the inconvenience to his pounding hard-on, he liked the way she said this: as if she cared for both their well-being. The objection was one neither he nor any fae he knew would have made. If faeries wanted, they took. If someone was hurt in the process, it usually wore off. Deep hurts were unpleasant, but at least they were rare.

Belle didn't like the idea of hurt. Her beautifully shaped brows were puckered with worry above her nose. Oddly touched, he stroked a strand of silken hair behind her ear. "What man would be stupid enough to leave you?"

She tossed her head haughtily. "Maybe I ended it with him."

"If he didn't please you, that was wise. A female like you deserves only the best lovers."

He supposed this wasn't something John Feeney would have said, or maybe she was unaccustomed to compliments. She squinted suspiciously as she stepped away, smoothing her hair over the same path he'd touched.

"I'll leave you to your business," she said, her green eyes narrowed.

Dubhghall fought an urge to smile. "Maybe you could bring me coffee. So I'll stay alert."

Her snort told him this seemed more in character to her. "I'll bring you coffee, but only because I'd like some too. Unlike some people, I didn't learn my manners at the zoo."

He did smile when she stumped down the stairs. Her departure was useful for more than entertaining him. First, he could figure out how to remove the showerhead without fumbling in front of her. Second, he wanted to add a little something to the repair—nothing coercive, just a small spell to tempt her farther into his net. What he needed from her, he couldn't steal. By fae law, it had to be won freely. He was glad seducing her would be no hardship. Earning humans' affections wasn't half as pleasant when you felt no pull to them.

His survey of the old pipes taken, Dubhghall opened John Feeney's toolbox to fish for what he needed. The ease with which the showerhead succumbed to his assault pleased him, as did the sound of Belle banging in the kitchen. She had spirit—not to mention the sort of passion he most enjoyed for love play.

He was whistling before he remembered he had no business liking her.

~

Belle was so shaken by John's kiss that she ground her precious New York City coffee beans into a nearly atomic powder.

"Sheesh," she muttered, snapping out of her distraction to shut off the grinder.

The man had kissed her was all. Yes, there'd been tongue and, yes, his strong hands had felt great on her, but Belle was no lamb to be reduced to quivers by someone palming her butt.

Don't forget his boner, she reminded.

When he'd rolled it against her, it had been as long and thick as she'd imagined.

The basket to Uncle Lucky's old percolator fell from her butter fingers and clattered on the floor. Thorough irritated, Belle picked it up and forced herself to concentrate on the task at hand.

When the coffee was ready, she sugared and creamed her own, debated within herself, then did the same to John's with a lighter hand. If he preferred it black, he could make it himself. He *looked* like someone who'd take it black, but she'd stubbornly doctored it anyway.

It occurred to her, as she carried both mugs upstairs, that John Feeney's presence had an upside. Annoying though he was, she hadn't thought about her uncle's eerily glowing work shed since the handyman arrived.

She found him standing in the claw foot tub, already fitting the showerhead back where it belonged. He was tall enough to do this without a ladder, though the extension of his arms and torso did make a fine picture. He'd rolled up the cuffs of his flannel shirt, baring corded male forearms.

Belle didn't think she'd ever seen a pair that sexy.

"I unclogged it," he said, twisting his head to her.

Belle told herself his quick completion of the job wasn't disappointing her.

"Here," she said, thrusting his mug toward him.

He climbed out of the tub and took it, moving into the hall with her. Totally at ease, he leaned one solid shoulder on the wall, lifted the mug, and drank. His eyebrows rose in surprise.

"This is great." He took another swallow. "Creating a brew this tasty requires talent."

He said *talent* like it had a capital *T*. Belle couldn't decide if she was vexed or pleased that she'd made it the way he liked.

"I'm glad you approve," she said tartly. "Coffee is about the only thing I cook besides grilled cheese sandwiches and scrambled eggs."

"Is that so?" He eyed her over the rim, a slight smile playing around his lips. Did he think she was implying she'd cook for him—as in, invite him to stay over through breakfast?

With some effort, Belle bit back a sharp retort. The possibility existed that she was oversensitive.

John took a stab at easing the tension, gesturing his mug at their surroundings. "I suppose your uncle was attached to this place."

"Very," she acknowledged, her shoulders relaxing marginally. "You're a local, so I guess you know he was a shut-in."

"Eccentric," John suggested, the teensiest bit of sympathy in his eyes.

"Who isn't?" Belle agreed wryly. "Uncle Lucky believed in some funny things." She shivered at the memory of the raspy voice she'd heard in the attic. Could the whisper have belonged to her relative? Assuming she'd really heard anything, of course.

"I gather he was a reader."

"A big one. Not that reading makes people weird, but his library includes some quirky books."

"He must have kept records. Of his thought processes and like that."

Belle stopped sipping her coffee to shoot her companion a sharp look. Why was a handyman curious about this?

"That sort of thing fascinates me," he said. "The mental tracks people follow when they're isolated. They stop thinking the way everyone else does."

Okay, so he was a handyman with an interest in psychology. Or maybe he knew this from personal experience. His wife and kids taking off might have made him feel isolated. Small towns could create a sense of fish-bowl self-consciousness. Everywhere you went, everybody knew your story.

He didn't seem self-conscious as he looked at her. His eyes were calm, his posture confident in the way of men who knew they were hot. Under that steady gaze, Belle's body warmed from more than the coffee. As if he sensed this, John's eyes darkened. Her fingers tightened on her mug handle.

"Are you free to come back tomorrow?" she asked, the need to send him packing before she did something stupid only part of what lay behind her question.

"I am," he said, the words oddly formal. "Your yard needs clearing, and the shingles on your roof are cupped."

Belle assumed this was bad. "Does my roof need replacing?"

"I'll have to look at it," he said gravely.

She should have minded that idea. Belle wasn't poor, but a repair like that had to cost. She had a mental flash of John, shirtless and sweaty, tacking shingles onto her slanted roof.

Evidently, this fantasy was compelling. Arousal welled and ran out of her pussy.

"Um," she said, resisting the urge to squeeze her thighs together. "What time would you like to come by?"

Her voice was husky. John's gaze dropped to her breasts, then rose to her face again. She concluded her nipples were visible. His expression was pure smolder.

"Early is good," he said.

His answer held such a purr that it struck her speechless. God, she wanted this man. Like, bad enough to throw him to the floor and tear off his clothes. Her pussy clenched, her better judgment at war with her impulse to check if he was hard. She didn't need to look. She could imagine fine, thank you.

"I'll see you tomorrow then," she croaked.

The smile that had been flirting around his mouth deepened. He handed her his empty mug. "Enjoy your shower, Belle. There should be plenty of pressure."

He was the pressure she was concerned about. He trotted down the stairs while she stood there watching, her tongue creeping helplessly to her lips. He didn't hesitate or glance back at her. Whatever he was feeling, she hadn't put him in a tizzy like he had her.

"Wait," she called as his big hand surrounded the doorknob.

He turned his upper body to face her. Even from the landing, she saw his eyes were blazing. He probably thought she was about to invite him to sleep with her.

"What should I pay you?" she clarified hastily. "We haven't discussed your rates."

She'd opened herself to ribbing with that question, but rather than take advantage, he cocked his head and considered her. "We can settle up when the job is done. I promise my fee won't be more than you're willing to pay."

That was an odd answer. Belle drew breath to suggest he be more specific, but the grin his gorgeous face broke into effectively silenced her. *Wow*, her hindbrain sighed. This man was a stunner.

"Don't worry, Belle," he said. "There's no extra charge for kisses."

~

Dubhghall was pleased with his exit line, so much so that he'd reached the end of her overgrown front path before remembering he had nowhere else to go. If he'd been in Faerie or Resurrection, he could have magically whipped up a shelter. Here, he was as homeless as an indigent.

"Fuck," he muttered in irritation. He didn't even have a coat.

He gazed longingly back at the bright warm house, then shrugged to himself. Charming Belle to invite him in violated rules he had to honor to win his prize. Roughing it for a night wouldn't kill him. He wet his lips, recalling the press of her little nipples against the gray sweatshirt. Hopefully, her attraction to him would keep *roughing it* to a minimum.

Because it was the closest cover he knew of, he returned to her uncle's abandoned alchemic shack. Though not heated, a careful exploration revealed it to be piped with running water. It was also wired for light, but he didn't turn that on. A small moth-eaten sofa would save him from sleeping on the floor. Though the ghost wasn't there to ask, he supposed Isaiah had used the sofa for naps. More evidence that he'd disliked leaving his esoteric labors was a supply of soup in a cabinet. Thanks to the peel-top cans, Dubhghall made a grateful if not gourmet meal of one.

Disgusting though the repast was, Dubhghall now owed Isaiah. He'd have to be sure to send him on to a higher plane before he left this realm.

Thoughts of his family rose as he curled up on the musty sofa, shivering a bit in the autumn chill. Dubhghall was the youngest of his parents' children, who totaled three boys and two girls. He'd grown up coddled by everyone, doing his best to avoid being insufferable—once he was old enough to know better. He loved his siblings, and their respect meant a lot to him. Finlay and Gavin were brave and fun, and no one could have defended the pipsqueak he'd been better than the twins, Effie and Mina. His parents, though busy ruling Talfryn, were fair and loving. Thanks to his mother and sisters, he had a high opinion of female kind. His mother would be aware he'd disappeared from their dimension, and would inform his father he needn't give in to Mor's extortion. Dubhghall—and his power—were safe beyond Mor's reach for now.

I'm glad, he told himself, wrapping his arms a little tighter around his ribs. A bit of loneliness and discomfort didn't matter. Humans believed deprivation built character. Maybe he was building his.

The shack's sole window suddenly went dark. Belle must have shut off the lights in her uncle's house.

Good night, he thought to her. *Dream sweetly if you dream of me.*

CHAPTER 3

T hanks to John Feeney, Belle enjoyed the best shower in the whole history of showers. The spray was hot and pounding, and the soap lathered like a dream. Her girly lotions and potions smelled better than usual, as if their scents had been created from real flowers yesterday. The hint of spice among the sweetness raised the possibility that John's to-die-for aftershave was lingering in the bathroom, but Belle elbowed that idea aside.

She was luxuriating here. No annoying males allowed.

Once she'd pulled on an oversized T-shirt and panties, she dove under the stack of quilts to stay warm. The fresh country air had good points. Though she normally tossed and turned, she fell asleep almost before her cheek hit the feather pillow.

The dream she fell into was one she'd had many times. She was in the rural K through 12 she and Danny had attended in Kingaken. Kids of different ages milled in the halls, and Belle was pushing her way through them. Her little brother was around the corner, or maybe up that stairwell. Sometimes in the dream her feet refused to go up the treads, because her shoes had mysteriously bonded with the floor. Sometimes she whispered a prayer she couldn't remember when she woke up. One thing never changed: the dream always ended before she found Danny.

Tonight the school felt more vivid than usual. She heard the hollow clang of lockers, smelled chalk dust and boys' sneakers. A bell rang, shrilling against her eardrums. The hall emptied of people except for her. She couldn't remember if this had happened before. She wished she could think of where *she* ought to go. Didn't she belong in any of those classrooms? If she searched them, would Danny be in one?

Someone touched her shoulder from behind.

She spun, thinking she'd finally achieved her goal, but the hand wasn't Danny's. Her new handyman faced her.

"Who are you looking for?" he asked. He was smiling, a pleasant friendly expression. Belle thought she ought to answer.

"My little brother. Do you know where he is?"

John sent his gaze around. "Not here, I don't think."

Belle's throat tightened. She ached from missing Danny. He was more than a brother, he was her friend, the only member of her family she could count on loving her. Her uncle thought girls were nitwits, and her parents—when they weren't wrapped up in their own concerns—weren't a hell of a lot better. Danny was the son. Belle was just the difficult daughter who liked her brother better than them. They were in agreement on that at least. That Danny also liked her better mystified her parents. They didn't understand it just felt nicer to love someone you could trust. Danny had known that, which was why him being gone was so hard.

But she'd be damned if she'd cry in front of a boy.

John touched her cheek gently. He was very tall. She had to look up to meet his dark gleaming eyes. That hardly ever happened. Belle was the tallest girl in her class.

"Why don't I take you somewhere you'll enjoy?" he suggested.

"I have to keep looking."

"Sometimes you only find what you're looking for when you stop."

"That's baloney."

"It's not baloney, it's metaphysics."

Belle wrinkled her nose. "You sound like my crazy uncle."

"That might be true, but I know whereof I speak." John took her hands and squeezed. His palms were warm. Belle felt as if they were shooting her full of courage, like maybe he was someone she could trust too. Shouldn't she give a boy this cute a chance?

"Could we go somewhere sunny?" she asked.

John smiled so brilliantly his teeth sparkled.

Before she could blink, they stood in a stunning desert under a blazing sun. Dunes stretched out from them in the vastness, a silent ocean spun of sand. The heat of the day was perfect, the rich blue hue of the sky. A large round tent had been set up behind her companion. Though its walls matched the sand in color, a painted band of cloth ringed its roof. The edge of the band was scalloped. When she squinted at its decoration, she saw pictures of very bendy people having sex.

"You're a sheik," she exclaimed, the conclusion inevitable to her.

John bowed to her like one. "As you wish, my quivering captive."

Well, that was strange. She'd fantasized about bondage a time or two. How had he known this was where her mind had gone?

"Come," he said, drawing her after him by the wrist.

At a wave of his hand, the door to the tent peeled back. Evidently, he was a sheik and a wizard too. The light inside was golden, and the air smelled of him. A thick suede floor lay between her feet and the sun-warmed sand. Heaps of pillows invited them to lie down.

"We're private here?" she asked.

"Unless you want to be watched."

She shook her head hastily.

"You don't have to be embarrassed." His skin seemed to twinkle in the amber light. "This is your dream. You can have anything you like."

It might be her dream, but even here she wasn't prepared to completely let down her guard. Once more she shook her head. John's lips curved with amusement, two deep dimples appearing in his cheeks. "Suppose I guess what you want instead?"

That idea she liked. A hard, hot pulse throbbed in her pussy as she nodded.

The sparkle on his skin flared higher, tiny rainbow glints jumping off of him. "Clothes away," he commanded.

Belle wasn't sure what she'd been wearing, only that she suddenly was naked. He was too, which made her inhale sharply.

"Gosh," she said. "You're really beautiful."

He was Michelangelo's *David* in warm flesh, a work of art so enticingly sculpted and buffed that his erection wasn't the first thing her gaze went to. His legs, his arms, the smoothly rippling muscles of his abs had her breath catching in her throat. His veins were more prominent in certain places: his neck, the lower plane of his abdomen, the bulge of his carved biceps. She experienced an odd desire to be a vampire, so she could literally eat him up.

Then she gave his hard-on a good look-see.

She had saved the best for last. Overcome, she pressed both sets of fingers against her mouth. John's shaft stood straight and strong, capped with a flaring head stretched taut by desire. To her, the deep pink flush on its skin was prettier than roses. Head filled with thoughts of what she wanted to do with it, Belle licked her lips and looked up at him.

His dark eyes were hooded, strange lights glinting beneath his lashes. She saw he enjoyed her admiring him. To judge by how his gaze traveled up and down her, he enjoyed looking at her too.

"Straps," he said, the word coming out a growl. "Leather. Bind her gently for me."

A flurry of snakelike shapes flew through the tent toward her: leather straps John had ordered to serve him. They slapped her skin and wrapped around it at wrists and ankles and knees, firmly spread-eagling her. The straps didn't hurt. They simply constrained and pulled. The way they looked on her body sent her heart up into her throat.

She seldom thought of herself as sexy, but somehow the leather turned her into a femme fatale. Her nipples felt sharp as diamonds, the blood within them coloring them ruby. It didn't matter that her breasts were small; the crisscrossed bindings framed them perfectly. She lifted her head to discover a sturdy frame had materialized around her. Steel eyebolts were screwed into the wooden uprights and crossbar. The ends of the leather tied themselves through the holes even as she watched.

Those were good knots. Belle wouldn't be able to get loose by tugging. An excitement she couldn't control thickened in her upper chest.

"I can't get free," she said breathlessly.

"You don't want to," John purred as he prowled to her. He held one final strap wound around his hands, the straight length between creating a snapping sound when he pulled sharply.

The noise cast a spell on her. Belle's pussy ached worse than she'd known it could. Because her ankles and knees were tied, she couldn't squeeze her thighs together. As her creamed welled up, nothing stopped it from running out of her.

John dropped to his knees in front of her, as if his legs had simply buckled. He was gazing directly at her sex.

"Do you like me like this?" she asked curiously.

"You're prettier than a rose," he declared.

When he put his mouth on her, it felt like all her nerves sprang to life at once.

"Oh my God," she groaned, squirming helplessly in her restraints. He was licking and sucking at the same time, focused almost entirely on her clitoris. Sensation rolled in waves up her pussy. Her thighs were trembling, her muscles strained. She tugged at her bonds, but only her hips would move. The leather held her like extra hands, the straps warm and conforming.

"Mmm," he hummed into her.

He didn't touch her except with his mouth. His wrists remained wrapped up in the last strap, as if he'd bound himself too. The walls of her sex felt like they were thick, her pleasure gathering in a ball. John rocked his chin to her harder, and she groaned at how close she was.

She didn't think it was *her* idea that the ties on her legs yanked them wider without warning.

She dangled at John's mercy, exposed and held captive by the skill of his lips and tongue. Turning his head, he caught the hood of her clitoris between his teeth. He tugged gently, and she cried out. Her climax had actually started, the sharp-sweet ache shooting up in her.

John backed off and sat on his heels.

"No," Belle panted, when her lips agreed to form anything but a curse. "You can't leave me hanging here."

"I want to." He grinned wickedly up at her.

"This is *my* dream."

"Which you invited me into. That means I get a say."

Belle knew she was pouting angrily. People couldn't invite each other into their dreams. Brains didn't work that way. "Even while I'm asleep, you're annoying me."

He rose to his feet laughing, the sound rolling rich and deep. He kissed her frowning lips, then nuzzled her ear sweetly. "Why don't you ask what I want?"

"What do you want?" she repeated ill naturedly.

"You," he said, "screaming with pleasure."

Having that to think about silenced her. He lifted his hands, demonstrating that they were still wrapped in the last leather tie.

"Unbind," he ordered, and the leather uncoiled from him.

"Are you a magician?" she asked.

"Not exactly."

"Then what?"

He gave her a mild scolding look. "Do you want me to make you scream or not?"

She squirmed in her bonds at the reminder. "Sure I do. I'd just like to know who I'm sleeping with."

"This is a dream. Who I am doesn't matter."

Belle would have debated this, except she noticed the final tie undulating like an eel in the air beside him. How was he doing that? She didn't see any wires. The floating tie made a little inquiring noise, as if asking John for instructions.

"Pleasure her," he said, not moving his gaze from hers. "But don't push her over the edge."

Belle let out a squeak as the tie slapped between her legs. Perhaps an inch wide and the same thickness as a belt, the leather wriggled until her labia made room for it. The tie's long tail wrapped twice around her waist, increasing the pressure it exerted as it rubbed her clitoris. The capper came when the front end tucked itself into the coil. Then her odd sexual aid really had leverage.

With a knowing smile, John watched her writhe and gasp. Belle couldn't deny she liked what the tie was doing. The smugness of his expression, on the other hand, she could have lived without. The most compliant woman in the world—which she was not—would have resented him telling it not to finish her.

"Are you going to stand there watching," she demanded between groans, "or are you man enough to help?"

He seemed immune to her taunt—too confident, she supposed. Rather than come closer, he slid his hands down his fine, fine torso and over his lean hipbones, teasing her with the beauty she was too tied up to reach. Sinews flickered among his muscles, mesmerizing her. Up his inner thighs he drew the caress, until his fingers supported the underside of his balls. Heat ran out of her as he rubbed their front with his thumbs. Belle marveled at the fact that even his testicles were attractive. What sort of man looked this good all over?

"I could do that for you," she offered breathlessly. "Maybe with my mouth?"

His cock jerked, a clear bead of fluid appearing at its hole. At least this part of him was affected by her words. The rest of him seemed determined to play aloof. He moved one hand to his shaft, stroking it lazily upward and letting go, upward and letting go, as if the way his cock stretched and shuddered didn't bother him at all. He looked like he could keep this up forever.

"I want your *other* mouth on my prick," he said, the hoarseness of his voice satisfying. "You're my prisoner, and I say you stay tied up until you come."

Belle let out a sound she couldn't swallow, the leather strap that sawed gently between her legs grown slick. "I want you inside me now."

The muscles of his face tightened. She knew he was affected then. Her wanting him was his turn on.

"I want you jammed inside me," she insisted, pressing her advantage. "I want you and only you fucking me."

He stepped to her, the motion not quite graceful. His skin was twinkling like a fourth of July sparkler, so bright it took concentration to see his expression behind the shine.

"Belle," he said, and then he kissed her.

He pushed her lips apart with his tongue, reaching deep and sucking. His hands came up to cover her hard-tipped breasts, causing Belle's spine to arch and feel like it was melting. His living touch was better than any toy. She threw herself into responding.

Her abandon seemed to startle him. When he pulled back to gasp for air, he was wide-eyed.

"Should I hide what you do to me?" she asked.

His hands contracted on her breasts, thumbs sweeping across her nipples. "Never. I want to know everything you're feeling."

He kissed her again more impassionedly, noises coming from his chest as their mouths dug into each other. He slid his hands around to her back, stroking her shoulders, massaging her vertebrae and her ass—probably her sexiest part, since you could actually tell she was female there. Though the ties and the wooden frame held her in the spread-out pose, his arms pulled her tight to him. She growled with pleasure as this allowed her to rub her belly along his cock. She rolled up on her toes to get every inch of him.

His satiny head left a little wet trail on her.

John ripped his mouth free of hers and cursed. "You are so tasty," he exclaimed.

He dipped to her breast and sealed his lips around her nipple, the strong pull of his cheeks sending heat streaking to her sex. Her breasts might be nothing to write home about, but her nipples were sensitive. Seeming to know this, his tongue fluttered over them with butterfly quickness. Belle cried out and arched closer to his mouth. He sucked harder, switched breasts, then went back to the first again.

"Mm," he moaned, his fingers kneading deeply into her butt muscles. "Shit, I can't drag this out anymore. I'm going to come in my fucking sleep." He tugged at the belt-like tie that covered her pussy. "*Release,*" he ordered impatiently.

The leather whipped away from her. Air rushed between her legs, cool against her heat and wetness, pointing up how open she abruptly was.

"Now?" she asked, loving that this brought his eyes up to hers.

"God, yes," he answered.

The rubbing of the belt had puffed up her labia. He ran his fingers between the tender folds, his gentle exploration slicked by her arousal. He sucked in a breath as his forefinger found and circled her hot button.

Not surprisingly, so did she.

"This is *good*," he said, his voice so basso it rumbled. He pinched the swelling, rolling it with enough pressure to make her squirm. Belle feared she'd have to urge him on again, but even he was ready for the next act.

Moving forward half a step brought his heaving chest to hers. They were almost eye to eye, since she was on her toes. The tip of his cock rested on her belly. John hooked it with his thumb, dragging it down her skin to tuck it into her folds.

His shape and her wetness naturally clung together. The up and down of his ribs quickened. Though she barely knew him, Belle couldn't remember feeling this intimate with anyone before.

"I want to move you," he whispered, "like you've never been moved before."

She didn't get a chance to answer. He shoved from the hips and filled her in one smooth stroke. That was delicious enough, but apparently, he thought he could get deeper. He pulled back a couple inches and shoved again.

Oh God, she thought, hands fisting on the ties that held her arms higher than her head. She needed something to hold onto. He felt so incredible, so thick and hot and perfect. Unable to resist, she worked her pelvis in a circle.

"Belle," John growled, drawing back and plunging in once more.

This time it felt like he touched her throat. He was in her as far as he could go, as far as her body would allow anyone. He slid his hand from the small of her back to cover her ass, clamping her tight to him.

Their eyes stared into each other. To her surprise, his expression was as dazed as she felt.

"Please," she said shyly. "Do that again."

The muscles of his face flickered. He liked her begging him. His growl had no words then, no more than his hungry grunts as he went at her. He fucked her like it had been a long time for him, like every thrust needed to be as good as he could make it. His hips struck so forcefully he lifted her off her feet.

His fervor was exactly what she'd been longing for.

She was being taken, unable to hold onto him except with the muscles inside her sex. Despite this, no man had ever felt this much *hers*. She knew no other woman was in his mind as he swelled more and went faster.

"Belle," he said, sweat flying as their bodies slapped. His face was tense, the slits of his eyes aflame. "Belle, come for me."

It was as much a plea as an order. She closed her eyes, savoring the slick hard drive of him inside her. Could she hang on? She felt as if she were half going already, but she wanted this to last. She chewed her lower lip, her neck arching back as she fought being overwhelmed. The strangest thing was, even though she'd screwed her eyelids shut, she could see him—as if she were both inside herself being fucked and outside watching him do it.

John's body was just as admirable from behind, his tight rear humping and grinding into her. The hand that wasn't locked on her bottom gripped one side of the bondage frame, presumably to help him keep his balance as he slung vigorously into her. The way his back muscles clenched was astonishing.

"Belle," he warned between gritted teeth. "It's been too long for me. You need to let go fast. I'm going to fucking go."

She saw something. Light glimmered along his back in rainbow colored waves, as if the northern lights were bursting out from his shoulder blades. The glimmers formed an ephemeral shape: two tall wings like a dragonfly's. John had wings? Why on earth would she imagine that? Belle had never wished her boyfriends could fly.

"*Please*," he snarled, slamming in and holding.

His plea drove Belle wholly back inside her body. Heat burst from him to her, his seed jetting on her walls. The orgasm this triggered was unlike any she'd ever had, every nerve from fingertips to clitoris seeming to spasm. Her pussy squeezed tight around his throbbing length, then relaxed, then squeezed, the involuntary flutter a pleasure in itself. She gasped for air as the sensations rose. Her head flung back. He slammed into her and ejaculated more . . .

Though she'd never screamed during sex before, Belle gave it up for him. John moaned like this was nirvana, his climax seeming to vault to a new level.

"Yes," he urged, suddenly churning in her like a crazy man. "*Yes*."

Hoping to catch a glimpse of his reaction, she opened her eyes again.

She found herself alone in a strange bedroom.

Okay, not strange exactly. She was in her Uncle Lucky's house, lying on her back underneath a smothering heap of quilts. The room was dark, quiet but for the rustle of leaves in the woods outside. She swallowed and her throat felt sore. Had she screamed in reality? The idea embarrassed her. Thank goodness she didn't have close neighbors.

Unnerved, she shoved off the covers and sat up. She was sweaty and trembling and pleasantly tender between her thighs—exactly as if she'd enjoyed an athletic lovemaking session. In truth, she felt so good it was a little like being drunk. Up till then, she'd thought only men could have climaxes from dreams. She hadn't expected the best orgasm of her life to be given to her in one.

Figures, she thought, shaking her head at the irony. Her first genuinely satisfying lover was a figment of her slumbering mind.

CHAPTER 4

D ubhghall didn't expect to dream-walk Belle. The spell he'd laid on her shower was only supposed to inspire carnal dreams. He'd hoped she'd cast him in them, but that wasn't guaranteed. Also not guaranteed was sharing influence in the dream. Usually, the host dominated, leaving the intruder to plod along. That hadn't happened last night. Dubhghall had gotten every bit as good as he gave.

He groaned and sat up, stretching muscles cramped from huddling on the small couch. At least the dream had warmed him enough to stay asleep. And no wonder, when making love to Belle had given him a bone-shaking double orgasm.

The strong scent of ephor warned him his clothes weren't in the same state as when he'd laid down. Grumbling, he cleaned up as well as he could in the shack's primitive washroom. Deciding it was too early to face more deprivation, he used some of his store of magic to warm the icy water and de-dust a ragged towel. His stomach growled, but he wasn't desperate enough to eat tinned soup again.

With an eye toward earning breakfast, Dubhghall searched out a rake and a wheelbarrow and started clearing the back yard. The house was silent, but with the sun breaching the horizon, it was light enough to work. He could always pretend he'd returned from "his" house before Belle awoke.

He made good progress. Even without magic, he was strong. In a few hours, he'd removed most of the dead growth, cut back a tangle of bushes large enough to have hidden more than one troll, and spied an actual glimmer of hope among the newly uncovered grass. Plants weren't as communicative in the mundane world as in Faerie, but Dubhghall perceived the locals' lightening mood. A nice little garden might develop here with coaxing, perhaps with some arbor roses or a created spring. A watercourse would have to be dug instead of magicked, but it would look no less pretty.

Caught up in his glow of satisfaction, he didn't realize Belle was awake until the back screen door creaked open. His heart gave a skip he wasn't familiar with.

Belle came down the stairs in a black turtleneck and jeans. She was a wand of a woman: straight, tall, her hair brushed back in a disciplined ponytail. The turtleneck made her look reserved, but weirdly sexy too. He knew the enchanted tigress the sober color hid.

Her expression was a mask as she thrust out a steaming mug—*his* coffee, apparently. "I fixed it the same as last time."

Her voice conveyed a take-it-or-leave-it challenge. Was she embarrassed to have done a boon for him? He tried to read her expression as he accepted the gift and sipped the delicious brew. As was usual for his kind, the touch of sugar gave him a little charge. He noticed Belle wasn't displaying the well-rested languor most women would have who'd enjoyed a stellar erotic dream.

"This is the way I like my coffee," he assured her.

She pulled a face, hugged herself, then surveyed the yard. "How long have you been out here working? It looks much better."

"Since dawn. There's life here yet. The plants were just feeling neglected."

She turned dubious eyes to him. "They were *feeling* neglected, were they?"

Dubhghall's grin sprang up without effort, though not without calculation. Women had been known to admire his dimples. "Don't you begin to languish when people neglect you?"

Belle snorted, but he could tell he'd amused her. "I suppose you think you've earned breakfast now."

"Wouldn't say no to it," he answered.

She *hmphed* again and turned back to the house. He took a second to admire her "booty"- as he believed it was called—encased in the worn denim. Belle hadn't flattered herself in her dream. Seen from the back, her ass was adorable.

"Well, come on," she said from the top of the steps. "It'll be finished soon enough."

She fixed him a simple meal with her own two hands. The scrambled eggs were a thousand times better than tinned soup. The French toast and maple syrup made him moan repeatedly with pleasure.

"Don't you cook for yourself?" Belle was regarding him with amusement over her second mug of coffee.

Dubhghall remembered he was supposed to be divorced and abandoned. "I mostly rely on food in cans." Because a technical truth didn't honor her efforts, he offered a confidence. "My mother used to make wonderful breakfasts for me and my siblings."

Those meals had been extravaganzas of her magical expertise. Dubhghall remembered swelling with pride that their mother was so skilled, and at the same time being childishly delighted. Talfryn's queen had a knack for the whimsical. It was part of what preserved their family as a family. They cherished who they were together. Unlike some fae, they didn't change themselves beyond recognition out of melancholy or restlessness.

Belle drew breath to speak, then hesitated. "Is your mother alive?"

"She is, but she doesn't live nearby."

"Mine moved to New Mexico," Belle said. "She and my father don't like the cold."

"And yet here you are." Without planning it, his voice had gone quiet and gentle. "Returned to the same town where your brother disappeared."

Dream-walking opened a window into another person's thoughts. He'd witnessed Belle's pain when she'd failed to find her brother at the school in her dream. He knew the complex feelings her parents' favoritism stirred. Belle looked into her coffee. She'd set the mug on the table, and both her hands clutched it. Dubhghall experienced an urge to rub her fingers but didn't think she'd want that.

"I ought to be able to let go. We lost Danny so long ago. I guess I just don't know how."

"And then your uncle left you his house."

"And then my uncle left me his house." She smiled crookedly, her grip relaxing.

Dubhghall thought about a house that always remained the same, that didn't grow new towers or rooms on its owner's whim. A house like her Uncle Lucky's must build up layers of memories. Faeries didn't do sympathy often, but he supposed some of his crept into his eyes. His earlier instinct had been correct. Belle grimaced and got up to put their dishes inside the sink.

"When you're done with the yard," she said, beginning to run water, "do you think you'd like to tackle the library? I don't really want Uncle Lucky's books, but other people might. You seem acquainted with the topics he was interested in. Maybe you could set aside the ones that are valuable."

She wasn't looking at him, and that bothered him more than he would have guessed. For a heartbeat he failed to notice she was handing him the access he wanted on a platter.

"I could do that for you," he acknowledged.

"Good." Her back and arm muscles busied themselves with washing the dirty dishes. He sensed she had more stored up to say. It came after she drew a breath. "Some of the books might be Danny's. If you find his name written in any, please don't put them in the for-sale pile."

He'd risen to his feet without planning to. Because he was there, he laid his hand gently on her arm. The stretchy cloth of the turtleneck didn't bar her warmth from him.

"I won't," he assured her.

She looked at him for a twinkling, the glance lasting long enough for him to see the feelings that haunted her. "Thank you," was all she said before turning to her task again.

~

Isaiah Lucke's library was squeezed into a small room on the first floor. The shelving was of varying vintages, built-in or bought from thrift stores as Belle's uncle ran out of space. Dubhghall took his time going through the collection.

Isaiah hadn't been as crazy as the residents of Kingaken assumed. From what Dubhghall could tell, he'd pieced together many of the principles of working magic. Actually putting them into practice was a different matter. Dubhghall didn't see how the old man could have accomplished that. The holes in his knowledge explained why the runes in the shed seemed off. They simply wouldn't have worked for a non-Talented human.

Except they had worked, which meant some other factor had been in play. Dubhghall was betting on Belle's little brother Danny. It couldn't be a coincidence that an interdimensional portal had been set up in the very yard from which the nine-year-old disappeared.

Dubhghall glanced at the library door. He heard Belle moving around in the living room, unpacking the boxes she'd shipped ahead of her from New York. She seemed to be tentatively—or maybe temporarily—settling into her uncle's place. Given her obsession with her missing brother, he doubted he ought to tell her Danny might be alive. He didn't know for sure what had happened to the boy, besides which she wasn't apt to believe his theory.

Belle didn't strike him as an especially open-minded mundane.

Not your business, he reminded himself. His business was discovering how the non-standard portal worked, plus charming from Belle what he needed to return home safely.

He forced himself to focus on a second survey of Isaiah's books, this time with an eye toward finding those that belonged to her brother. He sorted them into tidy piles as he went, a process that required little mental power. Faeries had an inborn knack for knowing what items had value, indicated by different kinds of tingling they felt through their fingertips. The minor magic worked fine in this dimension, without depleting his supply to any great degree. Dubhghall probably would have finished his assignment sooner if a book of Danny's hadn't sidetracked him. The first he'd come across, it happened to be an illustrated work of fiction concerning an elephant.

Enthralled by the first few pages, he pulled an armchair closer to the window so he could read without rushing. He'd give mundanes credit for one gift: they knew how to spin a tale. He hoped he'd get a chance to regale his siblings with this one.

He'd nearly memorized all the pictures when Belle opened the door and came in. "Wow," she said, looking at the stacks he'd sorted the books into. As her gaze reached him, his heart gave the funny flip he'd noticed in the yard before. Seeing what he'd been up to, her eyebrows rose. "You found Danny's copy of *Babar*. He made me read that to him a million times when he was little."

Dubhghall had drawn his feet up onto the armchair's cushion, but now put them back on the floor. "My apologies," he said. "I didn't mean to . . . slack off. I've never read this book before."

Belle laughed but not full out. She never did, that he could tell. "You're hardly slacking. I had no idea you'd get through this chore so fast."

Was he working too fast for a mundane?

"I have another shelf to go through," he said gravely.

"Okay. Whenever you're hungry, I picked up a couple salads at the grocery. I imagine Susi's mother made them, so they'll be good."

Her cheeks had turned faintly pink, which he thought both interesting and attractive. He recalled Susi's name from the ghost's account of Belle's doings. The owner of Kingaken's General Store was a local she'd expect John Feeney to know. "When do *you* wish to eat?"

"Well, I was going to eat now but, you know, you're not obliged to join me."

When she was flustered, she put unnecessary words in her sentences. She also reached behind her to smooth her barely mussed ponytail. Dubhghall came to his feet. He'd observed she found his height appealing.

"I'd like to join you, Belle," he said.

"Fine. I'll—" She looked at his mouth and appeared to forget what she meant to say. "I'll be in the kitchen, setting the table."

She spun and walked off stiffly, leaving Dubhghall with a surprising knot of heat in his groin. They'd only been talking, and he was hard. Luckily for his pride, she'd been aroused too. He'd thought seducing her would take more work, but possibly not trying was his best approach with Belle.

The flip side to that was that she didn't have to try hard to get to him.

They ate their lunch together in near silence. To his dismay, he enjoyed her company regardless.

~

Belle should have been able to forget that orgasm. It *had* only happened in a dream. No way would the real-life John Feeney be able to recreate it. Even if he could, she wasn't over ex and didn't plan to stay here, in any case.

Only a fool would start something up with an odd duck like her handyman.

If she hadn't found him lost in a storybook, she might have stuck to her guns. She didn't know many—make that *any*—grown men who'd have done that unself-consciously. His behavior was strange and sweet, and never mind how hot his long body looked curled up in that chair. Of course, everything about him was sexy: the way he forked tomatoes into his mouth, the messy spikes of hair that fell over his forehead. By the end of their quiet lunch, Belle was ready to rub herself on the chair.

When John got up to wash the dishes, not just set them in the sink, she was done for.

"Are you attracted to me?" she burst out.

He shut off the water and turned around. Belle sat at the old farmhouse table, her fingers clutching its edge. As tense as she was, she couldn't have seemed seductive.

"Yes," he said cautiously, his cheeks gone a shade darker. "Are you thinking you'd like us to have sex?"

"Just casually," she hastened to clarify. "I mean, obviously I think you're attractive, but you have issues and to be honest, so do I. Plus, I don't think I'll stay in Kingaken long. I'm definitely not looking for a boyfriend."

"Good to know," he said soberly. She had a feeling he thought her babbling was humorous.

"Right," she said, ignoring that. "I'm sure you're not looking for a girlfriend either. Plenty of women must throw themselves at you. We just seem to have chemistry, so I thought this could be, sort of—" She waved her hands, at a loss.

"Scratching a mutual itch?"

"*Yes*," she said, more grateful for his answer than was called for.

He was smiling, his gorgeous sinner's lips rolled together to keep his grin inside.

"Don't laugh at me," she complained. "I know you're prettier than I am."

"*I* don't know that," he said, his amusement softening. "Trust me, I'd much rather sleep with you than with a copy of myself."

She laughed through her nose, liking the way he teased. She also liked the way he dried his hands on the old dishtowel. His fingers were long and elegant.

"Were you thinking of scratching our itch now?" he asked. "Because, as you can see, that really would suit me."

He tossed the towel onto the counter, revealing that he had a lot more package than was normal. The bulge increased in volume before her very eyes, creases filling, zipper lifting, until she wasn't sure she'd ever drag her jaw off the floor. That was some stiffy he was sporting.

"Are you planning to answer this millennium?" he inquired.

"I think I need a minute more to drool," she said faintly.

His laugh at that was low and masculine, a lovely sound she hadn't heard in too long. "Come here," he said. "I want to show you I'm good for more than ogling."

He was good for a lot of things. He stripped her out of her clothes almost as quickly as his dream counterpart. Then he laid her down on the square tabletop.

"Take your clothes off too," she urged, tugging less effectively at his flannel shirt. The garment was a twin to the shirt he'd worn yesterday, but he smelled too good not to have changed. Chances were, he had a closet full of identical apparel, bought at

Sears, no doubt. Anything less like her ex's sartorial fuss was hard to imagine. She'd practically had to lock up her hair products around Tom. If John was an example of a real man, she was swearing off metrosexuals.

"God. Stop," John said at her continued fumbling over his buttons. He undid the final few himself, wrenching the sleeves from his well-honed arms. He wore a black T-shirt under that, which he peeled briskly over his head.

As he did, the muscles in his chest wall did truly eye-popping things. He had a scar on his left side that didn't look very old, but somehow that was sexy too. Maybe her handyman was a bad boy, getting into knife fights in backwoods bars. While Belle tried to roll her tongue back into her mouth, his long-fingered hands unfastened his trousers and unzipped. Somewhat to her surprise, he wore plain gray boxers. Given how hot he was, she'd expected something racier. On the other hand, perhaps he needed the extra room for his erection.

"Enough?" he asked hopefully, planting his palms to either side of her on the table. She realized he didn't want to undress more.

"The rest too, please?" She considered the lack of reliable heat in the kitchen. "Unless it's too cold for you."

"No, no," he denied. "I've bared you. I'm sure getting fully naked is the least I can do."

"*I'm* warm enough," she assured him as he shucked the dark green trousers down his long legs. Not wanting to miss the show, she propped herself on her elbows. He looked seriously cute in boxers and socks. A flush washed through her at the shape his erection made.

"You're drooling again," he teased.

"Only because that . . . thing is shoving out your shorts like a baseball bat."

He grinned and ran both thumbs inside his boxers' elastic waist. "If you keep it warm, I'm convinced the rest of me will follow."

Belle broke into a grin of her own. "I have a spot I believe will keep it hot."

He made a growly sound that stroked more than her eardrums. She impressed herself by remembering the very important thing she'd nearly forgotten.

"Um," she said before he could drop the boxers. "Not to be interruptive, but might you have a condom in those work trousers?"

A funny look crossed his face, so maybe he'd forgotten the need for this as well. He bent from the knees, picking up his pants to dig in their back pocket. His expression as he slowly slid his fingers in suggested he wasn't sure what he'd find. Did he fear he'd used up his lonely housewife stash on another job?

"Ah," he said before she could work up a sense of insult. His hand emerged, magician-like, with two square packets. Belle didn't recognize the brand, but that hardly mattered, considering.

"You *were* a boy scout," she said, deciding she was more grateful than annoyed.

"Or something," he said dryly.

Protection taken care of, he dropped the boxers without fanfare. He had a bit more pubic hair than she remembered from her dream. Other than that, his tightly knit body appeared the same: same beautiful thick penis, same veins, same tiny drop welling from its slit. She shivered from more than arousal as he rolled the protection on. If he started sparkling like he had then, she really would freak out.

"Okay?" John asked, rubbing her sprawled knees. He'd stepped to the table's edge, and his body heat was incredible.

"More than okay," she promised, ignoring her unsettling deja vu. She slid her hands up his muscled arms. "Come rub my itch, would you?"

His eyelids hooded a sexy look. "One itch rubbing coming up."

She caught his shaft in her fingers before he entered, wanting to feel him every way she could when he went in. Something about her caress turned him serious. His gaze held hers as his hips rocked ever so gradually forward.

He felt like paradise going into her—smooth and thick and pulsing with excitement. He moaned exactly as he had over her French toast, which she took as a compliment. His hips gave an extra forward rock at the end, ensuring he filled her completely.

"Mm," Belle said, loving that. Her spine wriggled on the table, her legs automatically wrapping him.

"Mm," he said back, lips curving as he smoothed wisps of hair from her forehead. As in her dream, she had the odd sensation that she'd never been so intimate with a man before.

Because this was an impression she thought better to throw off, she cocked her pelvis toward his. If he was like most men, the encouragement would get the main event started.

This assumption turned out to be incorrect.

John stilled her hip with one warm hand. "Impatient?"

"Maybe," she retorted, more unsettled than she wanted to let on.

He smiled and rocked into her again without withdrawing. "I think you'll like this better if I take charge."

Her pussy derailed her intended girl power anthem by convulsing around him.

"Fine," she said as he snorted in amusement. "Take charge if you want to be all he-man."

He kissed her until her annoyance bled away: slowly, deeply, tongue moving in and out in a sleek rhythm. Though the kiss itself was patient, the longer it drew out, the more his pulse and breathing sped, which caused hers to race in turn. By the time he began contracting his thigh muscles, both of them were moaning. He pressed into her in jolts, not really moving in and out, just upping that deep-seated pressure and letting it relax.

"God," she gasped, breaking the endless kiss to gulp for air.

John wedged his hands underneath her bottom, dragging open lips across her brow. "You feel good," he growled, keeping up the rock-and-ease. "You feel better than anything."

What she felt was insanely horny. Frustrated, she pressed her teeth to his shoulder, letting him feel their edge. To her delight, a shiver ran down his spine.

"I want to stand up," he said. "I want your weight to drive you down on my cock as far as possible."

This wasn't a plan she could argue with. "Do it."

He swung her up with a grunt that had as much to do with pleasure as effort.

"I like your Frigidaire," he announced.

Belle's confusion cleared when he pushed her butt and spine firmly against it. If this was how he meant to use it, she could learn to like the appliance too. Needing more to hold onto, she clutched his shoulders from behind.

"Don't worry," he murmured into her ear. "I promise not to let you fall."

The sting in her eyes came out of nowhere. She hid them against his neck and rubbed her hands up and down his back. A flash came to her of the twinkly wings from her dream. Even though it was silly, she gave in to her urge to explore his shoulder blades. The skin that wrapped them was smooth, but apparently they *were* a hot spot for him. He writhed against her, letting out a groan so low it seemed to vibrate her bones.

"Maybe . . . you should . . . stop doing that," he said.

"But you like it, and I like the way you're moving."

He cursed and writhed some more, his hips flexing powerfully. "You're asking for it, Belle."

"Yes, I really am," she agreed.

He laughed, and she laughed back, and then she found a place to massage on each scapula that truly drove him crazy.

He cried out and started thumping in and out of her, long hard strokes that hit her just how she needed it. The shelves began to rattle inside the fridge, causing her to fear for the bottles that sat on them. Really, though, who cared if they smashed everything? The pounding he was giving her was totally worth it.

She moaned as he shifted angles and brought her clit more firmly into the game. Her heels tried to dig deeper dents into his tight butt.

"We're going to break something," she warned him breathily, her inner cleaning expert compelled to bring this up.

He snarled and went faster. "I like the noise. It's exciting me."

"You're a . . . strange man, John Feeney."

"You've no idea, Belle Hobart."

An odd punch went through her when he said her name, as if it had some special power coming from his lips. Her body tightened and her climax jumped a hell of a lot closer. She didn't know why, but something made her sweep her hands all the way down and up his back, where wings would have lain if he'd had them.

"Shit," he gasped. "Belle."

She knew he'd begun to come from the way his hips suddenly jolted deep into her. He pulled halfway out and jammed his thumb over her clitoris at the same time. Her climax broke at the first hard rub. Something clunked over inside the fridge. Totally not caring, John slammed back in and shot hard. Instead of being dismayed, Belle made a sound some men might have termed a scream. A second climax had rolled over her first, building the pleasure impossibly.

She was still caterwauling when the incredible sensations swelled into what could have been a third.

Amazingly, given her distraction, she realized John was in the same state, shoving in and shoving in as if an engine with no shut off powered his hips. The pistoning was delicious for both of them. He groaned himself to hoarseness before he finally stopped.

"My God," he breathed, his brow resting on the freezer beside her head. "I didn't know my body could feel that much pleasure."

Belle hadn't either, not when the best climax of her life had happened in last night's dream. She was both glowy and unnerved. What she'd just experienced was more than an orgasm. To be truthful, it felt like a shot of unadulterated physical wellbeing. Maybe emotional wellbeing too—which she absolutely wasn't looking for. That way lay danger for girls like her. She'd count on herself for happiness, thank you.

Spooked and shaking, Belle let her legs unclamp and slide to the floor.

"Mmph," John said, bending his knees so he'd stay inside her. One hand rubbed her side and hip like they were old friends. "Give me half a minute. I'll carry you up to bed and stop you from shivering."

Belle's heart tightened at how wonderful that sounded. Too bad she wasn't shivering from the cold.

"You don't have to do that," she said lightly. She patted his arm before extricating herself from between his tall body and the fridge. He grimaced as his softening cock slipped out of her warmth. "You were great, John. Exactly what I needed. I guess I'll see you tomorrow."

He stared at her, then gave one slow blink. "You guess you'll see me tomorrow."

"If you're free. I'd understand if you have another job. If you're busy, maybe you can pencil me in for next week."

His heavy brows beetled together suspiciously. Sensing him trying to figure her out, Belle worked to smile brightly.

"I'm not in the habit of 'penciling,'" he said. Though he'd never removed his socks and now wore only them, he looked dignified nonetheless.

"Tomorrow then," she chirped like an idiot. "For sure."

He stared at her a moment longer. "For sure," he echoed grimly.

~

Dubhghall's mood wasn't pretty as he pulled his clothes back on. Now that Belle was gone, he felt every draft in the old kitchen. He was convinced his performance merited better thanks than she'd given him.

You were great, John, he mouthed to himself. *I'll see you tomorrow.*

She was supposed to invite him to stay over, to melt with gratitude and ask what else he might do for him. *Anything you want,* she was supposed to say. Everyone knew that's how it worked between faeries and humans. They were the lovers no woman could forget.

Unless . . .

He shook his head at the unlikely thought. Using his sexual prowess in this realm couldn't have hampered it. He'd felt his own pleasure more than ever. He could have sworn she did too. Damn it, the earth had moved for her!

He buttoned his flannel shirt with a muffled curse. According to the cracked oven clock, the hour was three in the afternoon. He had nothing to do and nowhere to go except wander in the woods. He didn't dare sneak back to her uncle's shack before dark. He didn't want her to know he was sleeping there.

You could stroll into town, he thought. *Charm some other woman to take you in.* He had to play by the rules with Belle. The rest of Kingaken's females were fair game.

He rubbed his sternum, resenting the way it ached. He wanted Belle. He *liked* her. Hell, he'd magicked a pair of condoms so she could sleep with him safely. If he hadn't liked her, he wouldn't have wasted his power that way. He thought back to her stroking his wings, which were only partly manifested in this dimension. Her touch had been caring as well as erotic.

The memory calmed him as he listened to her walking around upstairs, creaking the old floorboards. Unless his instincts had completely abandoned him, she was hiding from him up there. She liked him back. Her heart was just skittish.

He thought back to the "talk" shows his cousins in Resurrection had made him watch, claiming they were good research into life outside magic lands. Belle had what human experts called intimacy issues—and no wonder, given her history. If he was patient, she'd come around. Soon enough, he'd have everything he needed.

And then what? an annoying voice inside him asked.

As Dubhghall stalked out her front door, he decided he was not obliged to answer.

Chapter 5

B elle got next to nothing accomplished during the rest of the afternoon. She was too busy fuming and trying to blame her weaknesses on the handyman. John Feeney was too handsome and too damn good in bed. If he'd had a shred of decency, he wouldn't flaunt his unfairly alluring charms in front of females who couldn't defend against them.

That train of thought made her laugh. What man ever felt guilty for being too attractive? She wasn't even sure she could call what he did flaunting. For all she knew, he rolled out of bed looking like a god.

Tired of the war in her brain and between her legs—because, really, who wouldn't crave a repeat of their kitchen tryst?—she called Susi from her cell phone. The general store must have been open later than she remembered. Her call went straight to voicemail.

Crap, she thought at the loss of that distraction.

She tried doing laundry down in the dank cellar, only to discover the washer's tub wouldn't fill with water. To her layman's eye, the hoses and spigots were attached and turned correctly. Unfortunately, because the basement wasn't finished beyond stone walls and a cement floor, the process of checking the connections covered her in cobwebs and grime.

"Crap," she repeated, looking down at herself. These were the last pair of jeans she'd packed. Now she truly needed the machine to work. She'd have to call John Feeney whether she wanted to or not.

"You could call a real plumber," she muttered, certain she'd seen an ancient yellow pages in the kitchen.

A cold draft whooshed through the cellar, strong enough to stir Belle's ponytail. The air sounded as if it were whispering.

Belle, she thought it said. *Listen.*

The cellar's only light bulb buzzed and went out.

"Damn it," she snapped, spinning instinctively. She saw nothing behind her but darkness. The cellar was pitch black without the light, and she'd never find the fuse box. Not that this mattered. The bulb had sounded as if it died, not as if she needed to flip a breaker the other way.

The draft whooshed again, bungieing her heart up into her throat. Belle pressed her hand to the spot as a shiver crawled up her spine. Was that a glow over there, or were her eyes seeing afterimages in the dark? She had a powerful impulse to call for John.

No, she told herself firmly. *You're **not** that big a ninny.*

In addition to which, he wasn't around to hear.

Teeth gritted, body broken out in a chilly sweat, Belle stuck her arms out like a zombie and fumbled back to the stairs. Though it seemed to take an eon to bump through the basement junk, she doubted more than five minutes passed before she emerged into the kitchen. The lights were on there, suggesting she'd been right about the fuse. Her nerves calmed under the brightness. Old houses were drafty. That's all she'd heard down there.

She considered looking for a flashlight so she could replace the bulb, then decided to wait until daylight. Even non-ninnies were allowed some slack. With more force of will than tranquility, Belle fixed herself another grilled cheese dinner, ate four Oreos, and checked email on her cell phone.

Her assistant at Trusty Maids seemed to have everything in hand, so these entertainments didn't occupy her long. Her serial killer book appealed to her even less than the night before.

Tired in spite of her scare, she readied herself for bed. She was coming out of the bathroom when she noticed the door to Uncle Lucky's room was ajar. She was sure she'd shut it. His bedroom was colder than the others, and she hadn't wanted to waste the heat.

Sighing, she wondered if she needed to wedge it closed. She peered inside. The landing light was on, but the room itself was dark. Uncle Lucky's old iron bed put her in mind of TV shows about haunted prisons, so she tried not to look at it. The moon cast wiggling branch shadows on the floor. This drew her gaze to the windows, which was when she saw one of them was open a crack.

"Well, hell," she swore, stalking across the threadbare area rug. No wonder it was cold in here. John must have forgotten to turn the lock thingie on the sash. Country folk were notoriously lax about safety.

She'd tugged the window fully down and had started securing it when a hunched-over figure skulked into the yard below. Goose bumps rippled across her shoulders. Her cell phone was in the kitchen. She had to call 911. How long would help take to get here? Kingaken had a sheriff, but no resident police. They borrowed those from the next county.

"Crap, crap, crap," she whispered beneath her breath. Was it worth running around the house locking doors? Would any lock in the place keep out a serious intruder?

The man was doing something at the boarded-up door to her uncle's shack. Okay, maybe not so boarded up. The door swung open without trouble, the nails on the end of the two by fours apparently not attached. Clearly about to enter, the intruder glanced toward the bright half moon. Belle's mouth fell open. She recognized who it was. John Feeney was breaking into her property!

Anger surged into her as strongly as fear had. What the hell was he doing? And how dare he scare her that way! Forgetting her plan to call 911, Belle grabbed Uncle Lucky's Louisville Slugger and went to handle this herself.

~

The last thing Dubhghall expected was for someone to bang their fist on the work shed door. He'd been sitting on the couch, hugging a cushion to him in an attempt to stop shivering from his long tramp around the woods. Though he could have built a fire out there, he hadn't wanted to be spotted. Kingaken's wild places weren't as isolated as he was used to. It was a sign of his demoralization that Belle's angry voice perked him up.

"John Feeney!" she shouted. "Get your ass out here and explain yourself, or I swear I will use this bat on you."

He pushed up groaning and went to her. Thankfully, though she seemed plenty mad, she wasn't holding the bat like she meant to swing. "Hey, Belle," he said.

"Don't *Hey, Belle* me. What the hell do you think you're doing? This is my house."

Avoiding a lie was harder when someone asked a direct question. "I can't go home," he said truthfully.

"You can't stay here," she retorted. "It's a shed."

Since a fraction of the furious wind seemed to have left her sails, he continued in the same vein. "I like being close to you. I prefer it to going home."

The truth of Dubhghall's words surprised him. If he'd been lying, not only would it have temporarily queered his mojo, but a deception-induced migraine would now be splitting his skull. Instead, his head felt a little clearer, as if a veil had been peeled away.

Belle looked surprised for her own reasons.

"Okay, that's creepy," she said, much of the heat drained out of her tone. "Plus, it's too frakking cold to be playing stalker. You don't even have a coat."

Belle planted the end of the bat in the recovering grass. She didn't seem afraid of him, but more as if she didn't know how to handle her sympathy.

"You could invite me in," he suggested hopefully.

"You could go home!"

Dubhghall considered how to counter this argument. Strictly speaking, she thought he could. "You've no idea how empty a house feels without its family."

"Honestly?" she huffed, her temper suddenly hot again. "I don't know about empty houses? How about when the family's still living in it, but they check out on you anyway? My parents lost Danny, and I lost them. Not that they were really there for me before. They just gave up pretending once he was gone. Mourning is a great excuse for some people to be assholes."

He suspected she'd never said this out loud before. She trembled with the force of her pent-up grief and resentment. His heart twisted unexpectedly in his chest. How would he have borne it if his parents had treated him that way?

"Belle," he said softly.

"Hell. I shouldn't be . . ." She swiped a track of moisture from one cheek. "Look, I know you're hurting on account of your wife and kids. I'm certainly not trying to call you an asshole. The thing is, you can't let yourself go off the deep end this way. Acting crazy never made anyone saner."

He smiled, because the answer was so *her*. She wouldn't let herself fall apart, no matter what the people around her did.

"I'm serious," she said. "Get yourself back on a routine. As terrible as you're feeling, you can survive more than you think."

Fondness welled up inside him, warming him better than a bonfire. He was about to hug her—whether or not that was a smart idea—when he saw a glow coalescing in the dark behind her.

Shit, he thought with great energy. This wasn't a good time for Uncle Lucky to pay a call.

To his astonishment, the ghost was grinning at him.

~

Belle steeled herself against feeling any sorrier for John Feeney. Go down that road and before she knew it, him claiming he'd rather be close to her than go home would start sounding flattering. How likely was it to be true anyway? She was no fairy princess spun out of gossamer. She stood on her own two feet. Men didn't fall for women like her with that kind of intensity.

She was reminding herself this was cause to be grateful when John's eyes widened.

"No," he said, low and tight. "This isn't a good time."

The direction of his gaze said he wasn't speaking to her. She turned, expecting who knew what. An accomplice to his break-in? Had this been a crime after all? The blurry ball of light that hung in the air confused her. At first, the hovering sphere was small, like a spirit light from a photograph. Belle told herself she was seeing things even as the hairs on her arms stood up.

The light stretched into an oblong, brightened, and took the shape of a man.

"Hello, Belle," it said.

If you'd asked Belle that morning, she'd have sworn she didn't have the reaction in her. In her or no, she let out a full-on horror movie scream.

She stumbled backward, her legs too quivery to work right. John caught her against his chest as she moaned in terror. *Ninny!* the non-girly part of her accused.

"Shh," John said, his arms surprisingly cold. Their support was welcome all the same. "Let me take care of this."

"Belle," said the ghost of her Uncle Lucky. He'd been a handsome man in life—crazy Einstein hair aside. Seeming grave, he tugged his cardigan straighter from the hem, a habit she reluctantly remembered. "I'm glad you can see me. There are things I need to say to you."

Belle's teeth were chattering too hard to decline.

"You're scaring her," John said, his heart a steady thump behind her. "I'm sure that's not your intent."

"No," said the ghost. "But—"

"Enough," John interrupted. "Isaiah Bennington-Luckes, leave the earthly plane and rest for a nonce."

His order had the formality of a ritual. The semi-transparent figure shuddered. "Damn it," it said a second before it disappeared.

For a good long moment, all Belle could do was pant. Once she recovered, she wrenched away and slapped John across the face—another act she'd have sworn she'd go her whole life without performing.

"Ow," he said, hand to cheek. "Why did you do that?"

"I kn-now what a nonce is. If you could send him away, why didn't you make it forever?"

"I'm not the King of the Shades. I don't have the right to order him any more than I did."

"Are you even a handyman?" she demanded.

He paused an instant too long. "I fixed your shower, didn't I?"

"Why were you really hiding in my shed? Are you an undercover ghost chaser?"

"If I'm a ghost chaser, where's my crew?"

He had a point, but Belle didn't want to concede it. If nothing else, what had just happened proved there was more to John Feeney than met the eye.

What had just happened rushed back to her.

"Oh my God," she said as her anger ebbed and her knees resumed shaking. "I saw a ghost."

John caught her by the shoulders before she fell over. "Don't make me slap *you*," he warned. "You're not the first person to see one, and you won't be the last. As you said, people can survive more than they believe."

"I didn't *want* to see one," she said plaintively.

He let out a cross between a laugh and a snort, then swept her up into his arms.

"What are you doing?" she asked.

"What every woman wants at a time like this." He must have been right, because she didn't tell him to put her down. He strode across the yard with her.

"I'm not inviting you stay the night."

He opened the back porch door one-handed and smirked at her. "I think you are, Miss Hobart. Of the two of us, only I know a lick about shooing ghosts away."

"You'll stay on the couch."

"Honestly?" he said, one dark brow arching. "You'd sleep a wink with me as far from you as that?"

He had her, and he didn't even know how badly. Belle's body went as soft as taffy as he carried her inside and up the stairs to her room. His arms had warmed, and his eyes—though amused—were painfully kind. She doubted another man in the world could have made her feel safe after such a scare. They certainly wouldn't have tempted her to kiss them.

Belle made up her mind with surprisingly little struggle. Just this once, she'd trust another human being to look out for her.

~

To Belle's annoyance, John was only panting a little as he set her down on her bed. She was breathing harder than he was—but not from exertion.

"There you go," he said, looking around the way people do when they're in someone else's space. The turn of his head brought out the cords of his throat, which were long and lickable. His profile was so beautiful it shocked. His straight-cut nose, his full lips, his chin and his thick curled lashes all struck her as ideal—a toasty warm perfection that demanded to be touched.

Belle blushed when his attention returned to her.

"Would you like some hot tea?" he offered. "That can be calming after a shock."

Belle shook her head wordlessly. She wanted to ask a million questions—how long had *he* been seeing ghosts, for one—but even more than that she wanted him to ravish her. Putting the moves on him herself seemed both impossible and unappealing, an attitude that was as unlike her as slapping him had been. Belle knew how to be sexually assertive. Too assertive, Tom had used to complain. He didn't appreciate requests.

John sat on the bumpy chenille coverlet next to her. She was glad she'd made the bed that morning—at least she thought she was. "Cat hasn't got your tongue, has it?" he asked.

"No," she said, her voice coming out husky.

"Good." He reached behind her. She tensed, but all he did was pull the elastic band gently down the length of her ponytail. When her hair was free, he combed through it with his fingers, stroking wonderfully around her scalp and spreading the locks over her shoulders. Tingles ran strongly down her body from every point he touched.

She ended up as wet and squirmy as if he'd been stroking different parts.

Finished with her hair, he rubbed her back reassuringly. "A distraction would probably make you feel better."

He was dimpling at her, his outrageously handsome face inches away from hers. His delicious scent clouded around her, making it hard to think. Could he be the same man who'd sleep in a shed rather than return to an empty house? He seemed far too confident. Women ought to be lining up to offer him a bed. Mystified by his contradictions, Belle laid her palm on his lean, slightly bristled cheek.

"Who *are* you?" she murmured, only half to him.

"Does it really matter?" he murmured back.

She supposed it didn't, or not right then. With the sense that she was just giving in to fate, she leaned forward the short distance to mold her lips to his.

He sighed with pleasure, helping her press the smooth warm surfaces together. His muscled arms slid around her back. His body turned as he pulled her closer, falling back until she sprawled over him. She almost changed her mind about wanting to be ravished. On top of him truly was a nice place to be. His body undulated under her weight, and she couldn't resist the wordless invitation to rub herself along him.

"Mm," he moaned as her pelvis targeted his cock. His breath came faster, the bulge she writhed against growing. His hands cupped her bottom to pull her closer, one thighs scissoring between hers. His quadriceps were the perfect surface to get friction for her pussy.

"Belle," he gasped as she put her all into the motion. His spine arched and he wriggled.

"*Belle*," he said in a different tone. "What's this hard object I'm lying on?"

For a second or ten, Belle had absolutely no idea.

"Oh," she said, scrambling off him as her sensual fog lifted. "Sorry! I forgot I stuck that there."

He rolled off the offending spot, and she dug underneath the covers to remove Danny's composition book. Though she wasn't able to read it, she'd put it there because she'd felt better with it close by.

"May I?" John asked politely, holding out his hand for it.

"It's Latin," she said. "It was Danny's."

"I won't hurt it," he promised. "I speak a little Latin myself."

Of course he did. Didn't every handyman? Reluctant to release it, but not seeing a real reason to refuse, Belle passed the book over.

John was sitting up against the headboard now. Placing a pillow over his lap, he set Danny's book on it. One by one, he flipped through the pages, barely spending a second scanning them. Despite his speed, Belle got the impression he was taking in every word.

"Hm," he said once he'd reached the end.

"What does it say?"

His eyes were distant. They focused on her slowly. "Interesting things. Your uncle had quite the apprentice in your brother."

"What do you mean by that?"

"He made your brother his student in esoteric matters, and your brother seems to have surpassed him."

If she hadn't just seen a ghost, his mention of esoteric matters might have earned him a tart comment.

"Come on," was the best she could do. "My brother was *nine*."

"Youth can be an advantage. Children are natural magical thinkers. Being an adult, your uncle had to force his mental processes." John tapped the cover of the book where her brother had scrawled his name twenty years ago.

Though this topic made Belle uneasy, she had to ask. "Does Danny say what might have happened to him? Some cult or person he might have gone off with?"

"No," John answered slowly. "He doesn't say anything like that."

He twisted toward her nightstand, where she kept a small spiral notebook for jotting to-do notes that occurred to her in the night. He tore off the next clean page and wrote on it. Before Belle could read what it said, he folded the note in half, writing side inward, and slipped it into the nightstand drawer.

"What's that?" she asked, thoroughly curious now.

When he looked at her, his dark eyes were strangely sad. "That's my fee. At some point tonight, you're going to offer me anything I want. What I wrote down is my answer."

Belle's eyebrows shot toward her hairline. "Leaving your ego aside, most men don't charge for this."

He laughed breathily. "Not my fee for having sex. Making love to you is my pleasure. This is my fee for my handyman services. Don't worry. As I said before, I won't ask for more than you're willing to pay."

"And you never lie."

"Not if I can help it," he said.

The look in his eyes drove everything from her head. It was intent and smoldering and melancholy too.

This is the last time, she thought, searching his strange deep gaze. *He won't be back tomorrow.*

That was silly, considering he'd been hiding in her shed to stay close to her. Even so, she believed it.

~

Dubhghall had his answer. He knew how the non-standard portal worked. He could have rushed to the second part of his goal, could have driven Belle to the edge of so much ecstasy she couldn't help begging him. Dubhghall didn't want to do that. He wanted to take his time.

Belle was trembly and pretty, the next thing to a virgin in her unfamiliarity with powerful climaxes.

Her hand was rose petal smooth as he took it to coax her back on the bed. He rolled her under him and kissed her, reveling in her softness beneath his weight. His forearm cradled her neck, allowing them to taste each other in comfort. He ran his other palm under the fleece-lined sweatshirt he presumed she'd intended to sleep in. The front said *Harvard*, which he thought was a school. Much more interesting was the absence of a bra under it.

She gasped into his mouth as his fingers slid over her silky breast.

He broke the wet kiss to smile at her. "You're sensitive."

"Yes." She squirmed as his fingertips contracted gently on one nipple.

"Have you ever come from having your nipples sucked?"

She shook her head, the blush that sprang to her cheeks hardening him to the stinging point. John Feeney's trousers trapped his erection. Dubhghall had no hand free to adjust it. For the moment, he ignored his discomfort.

"I'm told it's a subtle sensation," he continued smoothly, watching the pupils of her eyes expand. "Not a hard climax like you might have if someone were fucking you and fingering your clitoris at the same time."

"I'm . . . sure I'd remember if it had happened."

He wanted to laugh at the break in her voice but restrained himself. With the tip of one finger he circled a taut nipple, causing it to bead harder. "I meant if I were to give you that sort of climax now, you'd have to pay attention."

"Oh," she said, her flush truly hectic. "I . . . well, I'm sure I'd pay attention if it was you doing it."

He covered her breast and squeezed. "Perhaps you could do me a favor first."

She swallowed. For a moment, he feared she'd say *anything you want*, and the game he was enjoying would be over. "What would you like me to do?" she asked.

Bless her and her caution.

"Unzip me," he said, his voice gravelly enough to pull a shiver up from her tailbone. "Reach into my trousers and shift my cock until it points up. Kissing you has gotten me so stiff I'm uncomfortable."

She bit her lip, a sudden grin trying to tug it from her teeth. "I think I can manage that."

She undid him with less fumbling than she'd demonstrated during their kitchen encounter. He knew faeries dazzled humans. They relied on the reaction when traveling in the mundane realm. Dubhghall liked that she was getting used to him.

He liked it even better when her slender hand slipped into his boxers.

He'd lifted his hips so she could move him. He'd hoped she'd stroke him, and Belle didn't disappoint. What he wasn't prepared for was how spine-tingly good it felt. She gripped his base and pulled up, not hard but firmly, allowing him to register her warm snug clasp on every millimeter of stretched skin. She pulled him again and yet again, his enjoyment building with each stroke.

"Gosh," she murmured, her thumb drawing a circle around his crest. "Your skin is as soft as a baby's butt."

Then she reached lower to cup his balls.

His head jerked back on his neck with pleasure. He couldn't speak, the air having solidified in his lungs.

"Does that feel good?" she asked.

"Unh," he grunted, shoving his pelvis toward her. Her fingers tightened around his sac. She was triggering his treasure-sense, the same that allowed him to sort her uncle's books by value. Her palm sent tingles rolling into his balls, as if *he* had hold of a rare diamond. He hadn't known those sensations could affect his body here. It felt absolutely delicious.

"Do that more," he ordered, his tone of command somewhat spoiled by his choppy breaths.

"What will you give me in return?" she purred.

A fae partner might have asked this to drive a bargain. He suspected Belle's intent was more playful. Just in case, he slitted his eyes at her, nudged her sweatshirt over the breast he held, and sealed his lips to her nipple.

"Mm," she moaned, his new favorite sound in the world.

He sucked her deeper, flicking his tongue over and around the bead. Her hand tightened on his cock, and he slid his own underneath her sweats into her panties. He stopped short of touching anything but her labia. Spreading his fingers in a V, he put a steady but unmoving pressure on her there.

"God," she gasped, twisting under his hold. She was so wet he had to maintain the pressure or risk his fingers slipping off the place he'd chosen. Belle's breath made an exciting whining sound. "You're really going to make me come just by sucking on my breasts?"

"Uh-huh," he said and switched to the other one.

It took ten minutes to fulfill his threat, every one of them memorable.

She drew a sharp breath before it happened, tensed, and then rolled over in one slow wave. Dubhghall sucked her harder to draw the soft climax out. When he let go, she pointed her toes and stretched.

Songs could have been written about her sigh.

Rising on his elbows, he smiled into her flushed face. He kept his hand on her labia, her heat and wetness apparent as she squirmed. For a human, her normally dark green eyes were bright. Her fingers came to toy with one of his shirt buttons.

"I see what you mean," she said. "That was nice but not intense. And it kind of makes me want a harder one right away."

"Does it *kind of?*"

"Shut up," she laughed, shoving his breastbone in revenge for his mockery.

He let her shove him far enough to tear off his outer and inner shirts, too hot for them anyway. Belle was fun with her confidence on the rise.

"So pretty," she murmured, trailing her fingers down his torso.

He rewarded her for that by dragging her baggy sweatpants off her legs, which went on for lovely miles. Belle shed her top herself. As she lay back, gloriously naked and *almost* abandoned, the white coverlet brought out the shades of rose in her skin.

"I like those clothes," he observed, rubbing her beautiful relaxed thighs. "They kept you nice and warm for me."

"Better than Victoria's secret?"

He gathered from her wagging brows that this was a joke. Unaware who Victoria was, he smiled and took her unresisting knees in his hands. He pulled them widely apart.

"Oh," she said, startled but interested.

Dubhghall grinned. "You did mention you wanted a harder climax right away."

"I did, but—"

He slung her right leg over his left shoulder, then did the same on the other side. He was sitting on his heels, and her hips were well off the bed.

"I'm off balance," she said breathily.

His hands were under her bottom, his fingertips massaging a knot of tension in the small of her back. Since she was in no danger of falling, he suspected her sense of being off balance wasn't physical.

Gratified for reasons that were very male, he lowered her and dropped onto his forearms. "Better?"

He growled the question against her mons. She wiggled, self-conscious about pushing her sex in his face the way she obviously wanted to.

"Um," she said. "Yes?"

Dubhghall solved her dilemma by planting his mouth on her. That was a pleasure that overwhelmed. She was nectar to him: her taste, her heat, her groans and squirms exciting him beyond bearing. His cock began to drip pre-ejaculate on the bed. He wanted her, but he wanted her pleasure more. Humans were so damn thrilling when they were aroused. Belle might have been the most thrilling he'd ever known.

Wanting to discover how aroused she could get, Dubhghall slipped his thumbs into her.

"Oh God," she groaned, her hands clutching at his hair. She was forgetting her inhibitions, urging him on with increasingly wild motions.

Loving that, he sucked her clit with more energy. The sweet spot on the front wall of her vagina swelled beneath the gently pressing pads of his thumbs. Her groans morphed into a strangled snarl, her hips very close to humping his mouth. He gave her G-spot a teeny bit more pressure.

"John," she cried, high and thin.

His thumbs were tingling. Evidently, his senses thought her sweet spot was a treasure too. He licked her little rod with the point of his tongue, determined to ignore his annoyance that she'd called out the name of another man.

"Please," she groaned, her head thrashing on the pillow. "Oh my G-od."

He licked lightly up her clit again.

He wasn't exerting sufficient pressure to make her come, though she did tremble on the verge. Her surprisingly strong thighs tightened on his ears. Dubhghall's blood roared under them like the sea.

"All right," she gasped. "I'll give you anything you want. Please stop torturing me."

The air rippled palpably—or palpably to him. She'd satisfied the conditions to seal their deal. He'd earned the prize he wanted. He should have been elated. Instead, he felt surly enough to smash something. Because Belle's orgasm was the closest item, he smashed it.

A scream tore from her as he sucked her clit in an inhumanly quick rhythm. The strength he used was as hard as he'd have employed on a fae. He knew it didn't hurt her. Her spine bowed off the bed, the brief scream stopping so she could gulp for air. Judging his timing to cool perfection, he depressed the vulnerable engorgement of her G-spot.

This time she wailed when she came, fluid spurting from her as she lost herself in the throes. Her sheath contracted so strongly on his thumbs he wasn't certain he could have pulled them out, even if he'd wanted to.

Grimly pleased, he milked her climax to the last tremor. Her enjoyment had a predictable effect on him. Stone hard, he released her hips, his cock shaking and aching with the immensity of his lust. He couldn't recall desiring a woman this ferociously before.

He was pretty sure he resented it.

Whatever his emotions, they showed on his face.

"Phew," Belle said, opening dazed eyes. Her expression changed as she got a look at him.

"Hey," she said so softly her voice was a caress. "Come here, you. Let me hold onto you."

He didn't know how she'd interpreted his reaction. No doubt she'd come up with an explanation that made sense for poor abandoned John Feeney.

He sank into her arms anyway, letting her pet him and stroke his hair.

"I don't know you well enough to guess what's going on with you," she said, "but I'm pretty sure your ex-wife was an idiot."

Dubhghall dug his arms underneath her until they were hugging each other. Despite his agonizing arousal, at that moment, holding her while she held him was all he wanted in the world.

"Sweet man," she crooned, the tiniest hint of a laugh in it. "Don't you know you're a genius-and-a-half in bed?"

She made him chuckle, which eased some of his anger. "You bring the genius out in me," he mumbled into her long hair.

"Hah," she said. "Me and the thousand other girls you've told that."

But Dubhghall was fae and could lie least of all to himself. Because of this, he knew she was his true inspirer.

~

Belle liked holding John, liked his weight and his solid muscles and the unexpectedly frantic pulse of his erection against her thigh. How could he snuggle her this sweetly when he was that aroused? Did he think she wasn't ready for more? Was he being extra considerate because he really did have a crush on her?

"I saved your second condom," she said, her voice fuzzy with pleasure. "It's in the nightstand drawer if you want it. I've never heard of *Tiger!* brand. Is it good?"

"Mmph," John said against her breast, his arms not loosening their hold on her.

Because he wasn't moving, Belle squirmed upward to sit. His cheek was turned sideways on her thigh then, his arms hugging her knees like she was a child's stuffed toy. Belle smiled even as her view of his muscular back and rear stole her breath. It really wasn't fair that he was cute *and* stunning.

Reluctant to dislodge him, she twisted around to open the nightstand drawer.

Something funny happened to her perceptions. The drawer began sliding out as she pulled, making the scraping noise old drawers do, and suddenly John's weight was simply gone from her. Between one blink and another, he'd moved from clinging to her legs to standing beside the bed with his hand slapped around her wrist to stop her.

He couldn't have moved as fast as he'd appeared to. Belle's brain must have been addled by her orgasm.

"I'll get the condom," he said.

His cheeks had flushed a red she'd never seen on them before. Belle gaped at him a second before her mind resumed clicking.

"You don't want me to read the note. You don't want me to know what I promised to pay you."

His face grew stormy but no less flushed. "We can deal with that later. We haven't finished what we started here."

She supposed they hadn't. His cock thrust thick and high from his groin, that crazy pulse she'd felt on her thigh making it wag mesmerizingly. Experiencing a need to calm him, Belle stroked his hip and looked up into his eyes. "All right, but—"

The front doorbell rang. John cursed in a language she didn't recognize.

Deciding this was a sign they needed to take a breather, Belle swung her legs over the side of the bed. "I'm sure it's Susi. I left a message for her earlier."

She found her sweatpants where he'd flung them across the floor.

"You don't have to answer," he said.

His arms were crossed. To her dismay, she saw her sweatshirt lying next to him on the bed. Mightily aroused and gleaming like a gladiator, he was too sexy in his anger to risk more proximity. Never mind his control, Belle didn't trust her own. Her sex quivered at the sight of him, urging her to attack. She yanked a fresh T-shirt from the bureau as the bell rang again.

"I do have to answer the door," she said, dressing awkwardly. "Susi is my only real friend in Kingaken."

John sat stubbornly on her bed, his formidable biceps still bulging, his scrumptious erection doing its best to impersonate a flagpole. "I'll wait here for you to come back."

Belle's knee-jerk reaction was to say *screw you* and kick him out. She restrained herself by a hair. Obnoxious though he was being, something in him called to her. He was wounded and moody and weird as all get out, but if there weren't more to him than that, she wouldn't be feeling this connection. One of her New York friends liked to say every girl-pot had a boy-lid.

God help her, but John Feeney might be hers.

"Suit yourself," she said with less temper than she usually would have shown. "But if it turns out there's pie, don't expect me to rush."

~

Susi had brought two pies and a chilled box of chardonnay. She displayed them proudly when Belle opened the door.

"Peach and apple," she said, beaming the same as if she hadn't been kept waiting for five minutes. One of Susi's best traits was her slowness to anger. "The apple pie is Mom's classic, but the peach is her latest recipe. It's fabtastic, I promise you."

Disarmed by her guest's bubbly humor, Belle stepped back and let her in.

"Kitchen?" Susi said, already headed there. "I know the old freak didn't have a microwave. He complained often enough about me selling those soups you heat up in one—as if no one should be allowed to buy them! Never tipped our boy Jaime when he drove the deliveries out here either. I'd have cut the old coot off if I hadn't worried he'd starve."

This was prattled good-naturedly. Belle hoped her uncle's ghost wasn't lingering invisibly. The last thing she wanted was for him to apparition or whatever around her friend. Blithely unaware that Uncle Lucky might take offense, Susi set her offerings on the kitchen table, then shrugged off her wool coat and draped it over a chair. Arms free, she looked around the place like a general taking stock of a country she planned to invade. "We'll warm these in the oven."

Strategy set, she turned back to Belle.

"Hey, girlfriend," she said, pulling her into a hug Belle found more comforting than she expected. Sleeping with John must have left her shaky. After a too-short embrace, Susi pushed back with a clucking sound. "Omigosh, you smell good! You've got to tell me what perfume you're wearing. I could totally make Hank crazy next date night."

Belle wasn't wearing perfume. She was wearing John Feeney's sweat—and her own, of course. "Um, maybe it's my shampoo."

"Your shampoo," Susi scoffed. "Fine. Keep your fancy New York secrets."

"I'll get plates and glasses," she said, not wanting Susi to spy her blush. She was happy to see her friend, but unsure she wanted to explain the John Feeney situation. She wondered how long she could count on him to stay upstairs.

As she searched cabinets for wineglasses, Susi bustled around with her own agenda, turning on the oven, opening the seal on the bargain brand chardonnay. "Sorry I didn't answer your call earlier. Jaime got into a fistfight at school, and I had to reassure the teacher his butt really would be tanned—after which I had to reassure Jaime I understood his position even if I was grounding him."

"Sure," Belle said, handing Susi two juice glasses for the wine, since her uncle seemed to have nothing fancier. "I understand. Actually, I . . . I wasn't certain you really wanted to strike things up again."

Susi let up on the wine box spigot and shot her a surprised look. "You're kidding, right? Don't you think I remember how fun it was to be friends with you?"

Had it been fun? Belle's memories of her childhood were overshadowed by Danny's disappearance, making it hard to be objective. "It *has* been a long time. And I never did answer your letters."

"Forget it." Susi plunked a half full juice glass in front the chair nearest Belle, taking the one with her coat on it for herself. "You're stuck with me as a BFF no matter what you do."

Belle sat and sipped, meaning to hide her eyes. Susi saw they'd welled up anyway.

"Oh honey," she said, covering Belle's hand like the mom she'd become. "I know it's hard for you to be back here."

Naturally, Susi's kindness made the tears overflow. "I'm okay. I just . . . I think I have a bad crush on John Feeney."

For once, her friend was struck speechless. Susi sat back and gaped at her.

"I know," Belle said, drying her cheeks with her palms. "Having a crush is so high school. And believe me, it hasn't escaped my notice what an odd duck he is."

"Odder than you know," Susi said, her voice a little strangled when she found it.

"He *is* good at his job," Belle said, unsure if she was defending John or her own poor judgment. "He's gotten a lot accomplished these last two days. I know his home situation is . . . delicate, but at least he's divorced."

"Belle," Susi said in the tone women use when they're about to break bad news. Belle's heart went cold in her chest.

"Oh God, he didn't lie about that, did he? He isn't still married?"

Susi put her second hand on top of Belle's. "John Feeney left town first thing in the morning the day after you arrived. I know this because he bought car snacks on his way out. He said he had a sudden urge to visit his brother in Utah."

Belle blinked. This wasn't what she'd thought Susi was going to tell her. "He must have come back."

"Not that I've heard. Besides which—" Susi hesitated. "Belle, unless your tastes are broader than I'm giving you credit for, you don't have a crush on John Feeney. The wife who left him was a good bit younger. He's in his late sixties."

"Late sixties?"

The John Feeney she knew was right around her age, but Susi's emphatic nod said there could be no mistake. Belle looked up at the ceiling. She understood how the three bears felt. Who the hell had been sleeping in her bed?

"Excuse me," she said, her voice echoing hollowly in her ears. "I need to go upstairs for a few minutes."

Chapter 6

D ubhghall rubbed his breastbone, no longer able to deny the reason it was aching.

"I'm not imagining it," he announced to the empty room. "I'm in love with Belle Hobart."

The soreness in his chest wasn't joined by one in his head, giving him the only validation of truth fae required. He loved Belle. He wanted to marry her.

He covered his face and groaned. Faeries had dalliances with humans. They didn't give their hearts to them. He had everything he needed to return home safely. He should go now, before Belle came back upstairs. She was, that very moment, speaking to a woman who knew the real John Feeney. Every minute he delayed increased his risk of discovery, and he wasn't a fan of awkwardness. Climbing out a window before Belle confronted him was the smartest course of action.

In his mind, he saw her reactions when he'd prevented her from opening the nightstand drawer: confusion, suspicion, hurt that he'd hide things from her. She'd fallen for him as surely as he had for her, and probably as reluctantly.

His mother liked to say every girl-flower had its boy-bee. She was the only fae he'd ever heard make the claim. Their kind didn't have many romantics.

"They have me," he murmured. His breath came out on a shaky sigh. The knowledge that he loved her didn't help him in any way.

Because he loved her, he knew the other reason he couldn't stay.

He didn't move when he heard her march up the stairs. Though he sensed her anger, every moment he had left with her was precious.

"Who *are* you?" she demanded from the door.

"I am called Duvall," he said, the closest pronunciation she'd understand. For a second, she appeared startled that he was answering. Then her anger returned.

"You're called Duvall," she huffed, fists planted on her hips.

"I didn't lie to you. You assumed I was John Feeney."

"Oh I *assumed*. I guess it's all right then." Her voice shook with fury as her eyes glittered with bright tears. Ironically, Dubhghall thought he'd never seen her so beautiful.

"Why?" she said. "I felt sorry for you. Why would you trick me?"

"I needed something only you could grant me."

She stared at him. He watched the memory of everyone who'd disappointed her scroll across her face. Her parents, her uncle, her ex . . . maybe even her brother. Dubhghall was very sorry to be added to that list.

And then comprehension dawned. "The note," she said. "The one you hid in the drawer."

He pulled it open, his dread that she would hate him no match for his need to play straight with her. A partial truth wasn't good enough. She deserved the whole. He retrieved the folded paper and handed it to her.

She opened it warily. "*I, Belle Hobart, having been bequeathed my uncle's worldly possessions, do grant the faerie known as Dubhghall all the names of Isaiah Luckes.*"

She looked up from her reading, her brows drawn together in perplexity. "What is this?"

"The truth."

"I'm supposed to believe you're a *faerie*? And that you want my uncle's names?"

"I have your uncle's names. You already ceded them to me."

"That's crazy!" she spluttered. "There's no such thing as faeries."

"You saw me use my faerie speed when you tried to open the drawer before. And that first night, after your shower, I dream-walked you. You wanted me to be a sheik. We were in a tent. I tied you up with magical leather straps. I can tell you everything we did, if you like. I promise you, I'll always remember it."

Belle had gone paper white. Fearing she might faint, he rose and caught her elbows. "You stroked my wings," he said huskily. "They don't manifest in the mundane world, but you knew exactly where they were."

~

Belle remembered that dream distinctly, including his tall and sparkly wings. She shook her head, trying to twist free of his hold on her arms. This insane story couldn't be true. Maybe she'd talked in her sleep and he'd overheard. Okay, strictly speaking, they hadn't *slept* together, but maybe he'd planted a bug in her room. He might have had any sort of equipment in his toolbox.

"Belle," he said, one hand rising to stroke the side of her face.

Belle gazed helplessly into his eyes. He was so beautiful, so dark and mysterious. She could demand he show her his faerie magic. That would debunk this nonsense once and for all.

Unless it wouldn't, a contrary part of her suggested.

"Why do you need Uncle Lucky's names?" she asked him instead.

"An enemy unearthed my truename. Faeries hide them, as a rule. With the right spell, truenames can be used to compel my people against their will. Once mine was known, I was vulnerable to being forced to do terrible things. Because I'm a powerful mage, this was no small danger. I had to flee or Mor, my enemy, would have blackmailed my father into handing over his country."

"His *country.*"

"My father is the king of Talfryn. I am his youngest son."

He said this with a perfectly straight face, a feat Belle couldn't have matched to save her life. "So you're a faerie prince?"

"I am. Though unlikely to inherit. My parents keep Talfryn in better order than most fae lands, thus making it a prize. If my father surrendered it to Mor to save me, all our citizens would suffer."

"You do realize how ludicrous this sounds."

"I have an inkling," he said dryly. He brought his hands to her shoulders, his thumbs rubbing them gently. The gesture disconcerted her, as did the fact that he remained naked.

Keeping her eyes on his, Belle drew a steadying breath. "You could show me your faerie magic, prove you are what you say."

Duvall or whoever he was let out a rasping laugh. "Sadly, I cannot spare the power for that display. I have just enough to get myself home again. My . . . batteries don't recharge in the mundane world as they do in Faerie. I probably shouldn't have spent as much magic here as I did."

Belle's eyebrows expressed her response to this.

"Yes," he said. "I realize that's a convenient excuse."

She didn't move when he smoothed her hair behind her shoulders. She should have, but the intensity of his gaze, the emotion it conveyed, was too arresting to tear her attention from. He gazed at her like he cared—more than cared, actually. He might be crazy, but she couldn't remember anyone looking at her this lovingly before.

"Do you *have* to leave?" she asked plaintively. The words slipped from her unplanned, causing her cheeks to sting the instant they were out.

Duvall cupped her face, his dark eyes gone luminous. "Belle, if my happiness were the only issue, I'd stay with you forever. You are the shining star that reigns over my yearning heart."

Belle's mouth fell open. This had to be the most ridiculous statement he'd made yet. "Duvall . . ." She trailed off, having very little idea how to continue. Did she want to warn him not to be so crazy? Or to confess that her heart yearned too?

"Belle, my kind find it highly uncomfortable to lie. You may trust what I say."

She wanted to—too much, she was certain.

"Everything okay up here?" Susi asked from the door in her best mom tone.

They both turned toward her. In Dubhghall's case, this presented Susi with quite the eyeful. She inhaled like she'd been slapped. "Oh. I didn't—Holy smokes." Susi's marital status didn't keep her from gawking . . . or gulping audibly. "Wow, you *do* look handy."

"Susi," Belle said, amused in spite of herself. "This is—" She hesitated a beat too long.

"Duvall," her companion said, offering his hand as casually as if he were dressed. No modesty problems there, she guessed. "My apologies for worrying you for your friend's safety."

"Sure." Dazed, Susi let him shake her arm up and down. "I take it the, um, confusion concerning your identity has been cleared up."

"As much as it can be. Would you be kind enough to hand me those work trousers?"

His pants were crumpled at Susi's feet. With understandable reluctance, she bent and passed them to him. The sight of John . . . *Duvall* dressing drove a lump up into Belle's throat.

"Duvall," she said. "Maybe you rushing off isn't a good idea."

"I fear I must." He retrieved his flannel shirt from where it had landed on the footboard, pulling that on as well. "Much time has passed already. I cannot predict how narrow my window of opportunity is."

He was talking funnier by the second, and she didn't like that at all. He sat on the bed to pull on his socks. His work boots followed in short order. Belle's hands curled into fists by her sides. Fully dressed then, he rose and came to her.

"I make no promises," he said. "Only that my heart is yours forever."

She knew she pulled a face. In her experience, *forever* was right up there with Santa

Claus.

As if he knew what she was thinking, he smiled, slid both arms behind her, and kissed her on the mouth. This was no polite peck. She had half a second to feel embarrassed about him Frenching her in front of Susi. After that, his seductive powers kicked in.

He'd tugged her right up against his warm hard front, the tightness of his arms pulling her to her toes. He was erect within those dark green trousers, the thick ridge beneath his zipper as firm as steel. That was distracting, but—truth be told—his lips were all he needed to conquer her.

His kiss denied her the chance to hide her reactions. Skilled though he was, he barely had to expend an effort to make her moan, to make her cling to him with all her strength and drive her tongue against his.

In too many ways that mattered, he was her dream man.

He turned his head to take her mouth from another angle, vanquishing hers anew. He tasted as good as he smelled, and greed swallowed her good sense. She wanted to make him come from her belly rubbing his cock, wanted to hear him gasp and feel the hot rush of seed. She caressed the outside of his leg with the inside of hers, a natural prelude to hooking her calf around his hip. When she did that, Duvall's hands engulfed her bottom, clamping snugly and pulling up.

The rock-hard length of his erection notched her labia through her sweats. His tongue pushed into her mouth—strong, sleek, slow—lingering for tantalizing seconds before it retreated.

She knew he meant to remind her how it felt to be fucked by him.

Perhaps he'd reminded himself as well. He let out a sound of longing as his mouth released hers. Belle's well kissed lips tingled crazily.

"Belle Hobart," he said, his hypnotizing eyes holding hers prisoner. "Do not follow me. What I do now is best for both of us."

His arms dropped from her, and he stepped back. She started to say his name.

"Sh." He lifted two fingers before his mouth. For a confusing instant, glitter made of light seemed to twinkle at their tips. "You are loved," he said. "Never forget that."

She watched him go with her heart pounding anxiously in her chest. Down the stairs his footsteps went, through the kitchen, out the creaking back screen door. Aluminum banged wood as it bounced shut behind him, a sound heard a thousand times that tonight rang with ominous finality.

That was wrong, wasn't it? Belle loved Duvall. She should be running after him. They could work out their differences. There were worse things than spending your life with a crazy man.

Spending it without him struck her as the biggest one.

She knew who he was at the core. Smart. Compassionate. Enough of a child to curl up with a storybook. Enough of an adult to finish any job he took on. And he *loved* her. No matter what his quirks, that was important.

She couldn't seem to make her legs do what she wanted. She sat back down on the bed and stared at the plain white wall.

Susi sat beside her and squeezed her hand. "It's okay, Belle. You aren't the only woman who'd let a man like that lie to you."

He doesn't lie, Belle thought, sure of it. Duvall just danced around the truth sometimes.

"The pies are warm," Susi volunteered. "I turned off the oven before I came up."

"Pie sounds good," Belle agreed, but neither of them moved for a while.

~

The clearing behind Belle's house was quiet. The trees rustled in the wind, and somewhere nearby a squirrel scrabbled up the bark of a trunk. Here in Belle's world, the monsters weren't those he was used to. Mundanes worried about mortgages and the price of gas, about keeping their children safe and countries that couldn't be magicked out of making war. These were no less serious hazards than goblins or evil spells, but if the human spirit could flourish among them, so could a fae's. Dubhghall dreaded facing life without Belle more than any of those perils.

He glanced back at the house's glowing windows, aware he needed to make haste before the spell he'd placed on Belle wore off. He closed his eyes and centered himself.

"Isaiah Bennington-Luckes," he murmured, "I summon you to me."

Because the name belonged to both of them for now, he felt an odd tug inside his core. The ghost came without a struggle, fully apparated by the time Dubhghall opened his eyes. The shade looked different from before, displaying more radiance and less individual personality. The barest outline of Isaiah's clothes and limbs remained.

"You've earned my help crossing over," Dubhghall said, "if that is what you wish."

The shade had enough humanity to scratch its temple. "I'm not sure your aid is necessary. I feel as if my business here might be done. I think my niece will be happy now."

Dubhghall wasn't going to contradict him, not if keeping his mouth shut meant Belle wouldn't be haunted anymore.

"I'm going after the boy," he said.

"That's good," the ghost responded. "I can't see him from where I am, but if anyone can find Danny, I know it's you."

If the former Isaiah couldn't see Danny, its reassurance was polite rather than factual. But there were worse things than politeness. Dubhghall appreciated the ghost's good will.

"Do you wish me to light the path for you?" he asked. "Once you see the way, you'll have no trouble traveling it on your own."

"That would be kind of you," the ghost agreed.

Belle's uncle was indeed close to crossing over. Illuminating his way didn't take much power. Dubhghall focused, and a soft new star appeared in the western sky. The shimmering arch that led to it began at Isaiah's feet.

"Oh," said the ghost, gaze turned upward, hands pressed over its heart. "*Thank you.*"

This was the only goodbye he got. The specter disconnected from the earthly plane as easily as a plug from a loose socket. One moment he was there, and the next the night itself seemed to have forgotten him. Dubhghall's new truename settled more strongly inside of him, shared no longer but solely his. Since that name originated here in the mundane world, the chance that any fae would discover it was doubtful.

Time to move on yourself, Dubhghall thought.

When it came to doing magic, intent was more important than ritual. Danny had understood this better than his mentor, who'd taught him just enough to get him into trouble. The boy had watched his uncle's failed attempts to activate the portal, then decided to give it a try himself. What he hadn't realized was that Isaiah, though an adult, was no safety net. Having succeeded in crossing dimensions, neither he nor his uncle could get him back.

Danny had described his plan in his old composition book. He'd supplement Isaiah's imperfect rune circle by burying objects at each corner of the shed, boyhood treasures with special value for him. One cache held a sparkly geode found in the woods, another a model muscle car he and a best friend had built from a kit. In the eastern cache, the power spot, he'd placed his most dearly held possession: a small stuffed bear four-year-old Belle had bought for him with her tiny allowance on the day he was born.

He'd slept with it so often most of its fuzz had worn off.

Danny had argued with himself for two pages that no other object would serve. He hadn't wanted to let Mr. Buttons go, not even for his grand adventure.

Coming from the passionate heart of a child, that sort of sacrifice had power.

No wonder Isaiah couldn't recreate Danny's method. In the end, the best he could do was board up the shack so no one else would be lost. That Dubhghall had gotten through the door from Resurrection was probably thanks to Mr. Buttons' lingering mojo.

None of this was suitable for sharing with Danny's sister. Assuming she'd believe him—which was assuming a lot—he refused to get her hopes up. Her brother had been gone a long time. He prayed Danny had landed in Faerie and not a hell dimension. Faerie—especially the wilder territories—held sufficient dangers for humans. Dubhghall himself would be far from safe, depending on where he had to search. He wasn't looking forward to it but didn't feel he had a choice.

Danny was Belle's lost treasure. If he were alive, she needed him back again.

Unable to put it off any longer, he entered the work shed.

He hadn't exaggerated about not having reserves to spare for proving he was a faerie. Fortunately, he had an ace tucked into his breast pocket: the curl of hair he'd liberated from Isaiah's baby book. Not only did the talisman contain sufficient power to open the portal, the Luckes family DNA it contained would help narrow his search for Danny.

Dubhghall's eyes had adjusted to the dark as well as they were going to. Careful not to smudge the markings, he stepped into the old chalk circle. He pulled out the little envelope with the lock, fingers tingling right through the waxed paper. This keepsake held quite a lot of juice, perhaps enough for one more safeguard. On the shed's dusty lab table lay a cotton rag. Dubhghall murmured a quick spell to it.

That seen to, he closed his eyes and focused. First, he needed to return to Faerie, to reassure his family he was no longer at risk from Mor. Then he wished to retrace Danny's trail through the dimensions, no matter how cold it had grown in two decades.

"Do my will," he whispered to the lock of hair.

"Do my will," he repeated to the spell circle.

Do my will, he said silently to his heart.

The runes on the floor lit up like neon. His heart didn't want to leave, but he forced it ruthlessly to obey. This was for her. So her spirit could be healed.

The tugging of the portal on all his cells increased. Brightness flared, a single saltwater drop rolling from his eye.

Belle, he thought.

And then he was gone.

~

Belle ate two bites of Susi's mom's peach pie, then had to set down her fork.

What was she doing, sitting here and eating? She needed to stop Duvall.

"Excuse me," she said to Susi. She scraped her chair back from the kitchen table so she could rise. Susi said something she didn't pause to answer. By the time she'd descended the back porch steps she was running.

Blue-white fire radiated all around the work shed, like it had the night Duvall first showed up.

No, she thought. She didn't know what the glow signified, but she suspected it was bad. Panting, she flung the door to the shack open, the glare so bright she had to shade her eyes with her forearm. After a moment's blindness, she saw rays of light bursting from a round pattern on the floor. She didn't see Duvall, but somehow she knew he'd gone *thataway*.

If she didn't follow, she'd lose him forever.

As easily as that, she snapped from doubt to faith. Duvall was a faerie. She needed to go into that light after him.

She'd run outside in her sweat clothes and socks. As if she were an Olympic long jumper, she leaped from the door to the brilliant circle, terrified but not caring.

The light immediately dimmed by half.

She thought her socks must have scuffed the marks. That was never good when people did magic on TV shows.

Then she saw the rag.

Seemingly by itself, it was busily wiping out the spell circle around her, like the enchanted mop and bucket from *The Sorcerer's Apprentice*. Though she tried to grab it, it evaded her. In seconds, the light went out completely.

Belle breathed raggedly in shock, her blood roaring in her ears. The shed was empty. Through the single window, light shone secondhand from the house. Rubbed-out chalk smeared the planks she stood on. The rag laid still, an inanimate cloth once more. It had done its job so well she had no clue what the original pattern was.

She had a feeling that was no accident.

"Duvall," she gasped, her throat clogging up with tears she hadn't begun to shed.

Her beloved didn't answer—couldn't, she supposed. Like her brother so long ago, he wasn't there to hear. Also like her brother, she had no way to follow him.

CHAPTER 7

B elle hadn't planned on staying in Kingaken. For the first few days after Duvall disappeared through the magic door, she was too wrecked to drive to Manhattan. How could she, when she'd have to pull over every twenty minutes to sob her heart out again. When that mortifying trend wore off, she tried reminding herself Kingaken wasn't home any more. She had two sets of bad memories here, three if you counted her folks not being model parents even before Danny disappeared. A sensible person would have headed back to the concrete hills.

As the weeks drew out and she still hadn't packed her suitcase, Belle concluded the world of sensible people didn't include her.

When the real John Feeney returned from his trip to Utah, Belle hired him to finish the fixing-up Duvall had started. John Feeney wasn't as easy on the eye as his imitator—or as charming. On the plus side, his handyman skills appeared to have been earned honestly. Together with his equally curmudgeonly—but not divorced—cousin Bob, they painted the siding, replaced the roof, rehabbed the shutters, cleared the front yard, and dug a little fish pond she thought would be nice to sit by come spring.

In a strange way, Susi's original prediction had been correct. She and John Feeney did hit it off. His grumpy but not ill meaning company was exactly what Belle needed. His presence reassured her she was a part of life without expecting too much of her in return. By the time the first real snow blanketed the Catskills, she let Susi convince her to join a girls' night out.

Girls' night in Kingaken involved bowling, beer, and no small amount of good-natured griping about husbands and children. Considering Belle had neither, she should have hated it—or at least felt alien. Instead, she found the evening soothing. Susi's friends were good people, and Susi herself had depths Belle had been too young to appreciate twenty years ago. Susi didn't push Belle. She let Belle take her own time recovering.

Bit by bit, Belle progressed in her therapy. She cleared the furniture from Uncle Lucky's bedroom so it could be painted, then bought some antiques she liked better to move back in. With a coat of soft blue-gray on the walls, it hardly seemed this had been his space. She didn't sense his presence around the house, haunting or otherwise.

It seemed he'd accomplished whatever he'd come back for.

Duvall's presence, by contrast, seemed to have soaked into every board and nail. She smelled him on the sheets even after she washed them. She remembered how his footsteps sounded, the feel of his arms around her, the clear-cut beauty of his profile. None of the memories faded. They were as vivid after a month as they'd been that first day.

Possibly the fact that this made her happy meant she was wrong in the head. Belle didn't care if it did. *You are loved,* he'd said. *Never forget that.*

As long as she stayed here, she wasn't able to.

Once two months had passed, she sold her rent-a-maid business in New York to her eager-beaver assistant. As she continued to make Isaiah's house her own, ideas began to come to her of businesses that could succeed here. Kingaken might be feeling the pinch these days, but Belle doubted that pinch would last forever. This town had been here too long. Like her, when the going got tough, Kingaken dug its heels in and got stubborn.

Belle pretty much loved that.

The mountain snowfalls grew heavier, turning Kingaken into a Grandma Moses painting and Belle into a lover of her wood-burning fireplace. Susi's fourteen-year-old son came by to help her hang Christmas lights. Occasional fistfight aside, Jaime was a nice kid.

"You should have a tree," he said, his husky arms loaded with firewood he'd helped her split. "A real one. Mom's making me get you a present."

Apparently, if he had to get her a present, he wanted a decent shelter for it to sit under.

"I haven't had a real tree in twenty years," Belle said, amused and startled by his idea. Her parents stopped doing Christmas after Danny disappeared. Almost as bad, the two years she and Tom had lived together, he'd insisted on "tasteful" white tinsel with all-white ornaments.

Jaime dropped the firewood into its holder, after which she and he stood shoulder to shoulder, contemplating the spot in her living room where a real Douglas fir would fit.

"We'd come by," Jaime said, clearly meaning his family. "Maybe for Christmas Eve. You could bake cookies and serve eggnog. Then, if you wanted, you could come with us to church. The sermon's generally okay, and singing with the choir is fun."

When it came to apples, Jaime's didn't fall too far from the tree. Belle saw he'd adopted her into his circle of loved ones as easily as his mom. She had to clear her throat before she could speak. "It might be safer if I bribed your grandmother to bake for me."

"Grandma J would like teaching you better. She never gets bored of having pupils. Plus, if you made at least one batch yourself, the house will smell like it should."

Not wanting Jaime to feel uncomfortable, Belle wiped away the tear track that was trickling down her face.

"You have a point," she said. Duvall had smelled like Christmas: spicy and sweet. Plus, he'd sparkled like the holidays. Smiling at that, Belle decided. "All right. I'll host cookies and eggnog for Christmas Eve. I warn you, though, I'll be inviting John Feeney."

Jaime groaned, but he was grinning.

This is good, Belle thought. *This is more than coming back to life again.*

~

Susi's mother, aka Grandma J, was as quirky as Belle recalled. She was so passionate on the subject of baking that she sometimes sounded as if she were discussing sex. The blue ribbons she'd won at fairs filled numerous shoeboxes, her entries often inspiring judges to return for seconds. On the Friday before Christmas, she arrived at Belle's place with two canvas totes bulging with supplies. Belle had bought flour and such, per instructions, so these supplies were tools. Belle suspected

Mrs. J had scoured every junk shop in thirty miles for them.

Though she was as short as her daughter, Mrs. J was strong. She clucked her tongue at Belle's attempt to take the heavy bags from her.

"This is your Christmas present," she said, carrying them to the kitchen. "And your housewarming. Secondhand is fine for baking, but you need the right equipment for good results—which I happen to know your uncle never bothered with."

Isaiah's old electric stove made her thunk the bags on the table and shake her head. "You need a real oven if you're going to get serious about this. I'll keep an eye out for one on eBay."

Mrs. J seemed to take her getting serious as a foregone conclusion.

"I saw that eye roll," she warned, nodding her permission for Belle to start unpacking. "I'll have you know, baking is a great way to catch a man, especially these days. People love feeling cared for that way. Also, faeries have terrible sweet tooths."

Belle nearly dropped the beaters for a stand mixer. The floor beneath her riding boots seemed to rock. "Excuse me?"

Mrs. J broke into a brilliant smile. "Faeries love sweets. And orange juice makes them tipsy. Susi told me about that character 'Duvall' who pretended to be John Feeney and then took off. When she said how pretty he was, I figured I knew what was what."

Belle pulled out a chair and sat heavily on it. "Susi didn't say a word."

"Susi doesn't know what she saw, but when I was seventeen, one of Them turned my world upside down." She sat down herself, smiling kindly across the appliance-strewn table. "No one but a faerie could steal a girl's heart so fast. Mind you, they can't be kept unless they want to be, but—oh my—what a ride before they go!"

She laughed with her hand pressed to her bosom, entertained by her memories. Her blue eyes twinkled as brightly as a woman's half her age.

"You married," Belle said.

"Sure I did. And I love my husband. That doesn't mean I can't keep a naughty dream or two to myself."

Belle considered this. "I don't think I could do that," she said slowly. "I think I gave him my heart for good."

Mrs. J patted Belle's hand the same way her daughter would have. "So be it then. As long as you don't spend your whole life moping, you've a right to your own choices."

Belle thought about that too. Her body felt lighter, as if saying the truth aloud had lifted off a burden. "I'm glad you shared this with me."

Mrs. J's smile turned rueful. "I almost talked about it after Danny went missing. In stories, the fair folk do sometimes steal children."

"No one would have believed you. And what good would it have done if they had? My uncle was nuts enough to believe, but he couldn't get Danny back."

Mrs. J heaved a sigh of acknowledgment. "So," she said, pushing to her feet again. "Let's see what that junky old stove can do."

It could do quite a lot with Mrs. J babying it. Belle watched what she did as closely as she could, what with the other intriguing topic she'd given her to mull over. Faeries had traveled to Kingaken before, with or without her uncle's help. Maybe Isaiah had heard stories, and they'd sparked his seemingly off-the-wall fixation. The idea of pursuing the same path that he had didn't seem very smart. Hoping, though, might not be as deluded as she'd thought.

~

Belle decided there was nothing like a crackling fire and a living room full of laughing people. Susi and her family were at her house for Christmas Eve afternoon. John Feeney had shown up, plus—surprisingly enough—his laconic cousin Bob and his humorously broody brood. Some interesting blushes were being exchanged between Jaime and Bob's slightly less surly teenage daughter. She'd turned a hand-knitted reindeer sweater into a punk masterpiece with nothing more than a pair of scissors and many safety pins. Belle and Mrs. J had baked a mountain of sweets, and Belle's solo effort at pecan drop cookies thankfully passed muster. Preparing the homemade eggnog was a breeze by comparison. Susi's husband spiked it with rum for the adults, and even dour John Feeney grew cheerful after a cup of it.

Belle was cheerful herself. Her last-minute wardrobe choice was the skimpy dress she'd found in the attic the night she and Duvall met. Because the neckline was a bit *aiyiyi* for a family gathering, she'd paired it with a black cardigan. The vintage silk caressed her underneath, her secret reminder of sweetness.

To make the day truly perfect, a gentle snow fell outside the icicle-draped windows.

"Your tree is so beautiful!" Susi exclaimed for the umpteenth time. "Those antique ornaments are genius."

"Finding them at the secondhand shops was fun. Of all the businesses around here, they seem to be doing well." Belle paused, her heart rate accelerating in anticipation of her announcement. She strove to sound casual. "I'm thinking I might start my own."

Susi had been petting her six-year-old daughter's hair and watching the tree. Now she turned her full wide-eyed attention onto Belle. "Really?"

"Your mom said she'd let me hire her for consulting."

"Mom!" Susi exclaimed, giving her mother's plump knee a smack. "You might have said."

"I don't tell you everything, dear," Mrs. J said calmly.

Mr. J expressed his hope that this would result in his wife spending a few less hours per month baking pies, not realizing Belle was hoping to sell them in her future shop. Faeries weren't the only ones who'd consider them a draw.

"But this means Belle is staying!" Susi said. "It's such wonderful news."

If her daughter hadn't been curled up in her lap, Belle was sure she'd have hopped up to hug her.

"I'm glad you're glad," Belle said. "You're a big part of the reason why. The city has its perks, but I missed my BFF."

"Aw," Susi said. "You're going to make me cry."

Jaime groaned teenager-style as the doorbell rang. A tingle swept Belle's body, as if a sparkling wave of snow were being blown across her skin.

"Did you invite someone else?" Susi asked curiously.

"No." Belle had been leaning on the back of the leather couch, wanting to leave the seats for guests. When she turned to face the door, nothing but a rag rug lay between her and it.

Don't get your hopes up, she warned as a pulse sprang up in her throat. Never mind she'd dressed for the man who had won her heart. She didn't have a single reason to think Duvall would—or even could—come back.

"Well, *answer* it," Bob's retro-punk daughter Carly joked. "Maybe it's the spirit of Christmas past."

Calling herself an idiot, Belle did as she was advised.

For the second time since she'd returned to Kingaken, she found a stranger on her front porch.

He stood over six foot tall and was bundled for cold weather in a dark wool coat and striped scarf. He had a wonderful face—not handsome, exactly, but full of character and intelligence, giving the impression of a young man with an old soul. She glanced behind him, but didn't see another car. He must have walked up the steep tree-lined drive, though his long lanky legs would make that less of a chore. Snow had collected on his brown hair, which fell to wide shoulders. He swept the white off with leather gloves, his grin baring bright, slightly gapped front teeth.

"Hey, Tinker Belle," he said.

Belle gasped at the familiarity of his voice—and the nearly forgotten nickname. "Danny?" she managed to croak out.

She probably came the closest she ever had to fainting.

He caught her into a bear hug, sparing her from discovering what that was like. He'd gotten so big, not a skinny squirt anymore. Both of them were crying as they embraced. Despite the tears, joy fizzed like champagne inside her. This was Danny. Her brother had come back to her.

"How can it be you?" Belle pushed back far enough to see his miraculous grown-up face. Now that she was looking, she could see the nine-year-old in his features: the bright green eyes lit up by her porch light, the scattering of freckles on the bridge of his ski slope nose. He looked more like their father than she did, but his hair was the same chestnut brown as hers, ruler straight and impossible to style.

He smiled, taking in the changes in her as well. "It's a long story," he said, sounding tired as he brushed her tears off with the thumb of his glove. "One I'm going to have to tell you privately."

He shot a meaningful glance behind her. Belle belatedly realized they had a very attentive audience peering out from the living room. She let out a breathy laugh. "I hope you have *something* up your sleeve to tell them. They're not going to let you off without answering."

Danny did have a tale prepared, and fortunately he'd always been a convincing liar. Apart from Bob Feeney's wife and kids, everyone knew at least vaguely who Danny was. His mysterious disappearance had been big news in the tiny town. He confirmed what had been a popular if farfetched theory: that a couple of tourists who'd lost a child spotted him in Isaiah's yard while they were hiking through the woods. Reminded of the son who'd died, they'd abducted him, keeping him a virtual prisoner in their remote Colorado home. Danny said he hadn't been mistreated, and eventually he'd adjusted. Only when the couple were killed in an accident did he decide to see if he could come home.

"Wow," Carly Feeney said once he'd finished. "That is, like, wicked weird. Nobody would believe it if it hadn't actually happened."

"I expect not," Danny said wryly. "I hope people will understand if I don't want to talk about it too much."

Everyone exclaimed that of course they did, a politeness Belle doubted anyone really meant. The pretense served their purposes well enough. After shedding his coat and accepting a quick round of hugs from Susi's relations, she and Danny escaped upstairs.

As if they were still kids, they clutched each other's hands all the way to the second floor. Letting go at the landing, Danny walked into Uncle Lucky's former room, where he sat somewhat absently on the bed. Belle shut the door so they would have privacy.

"This is different," he said, gripping the mattress edge with a nervousness she recognized from way back—usually when *she* was about to catch hell from their parents for some misdeed. His eyes took a tour of the furnishings before coming back to her. "I guess the old coot left the place to you."

"He would have left it to you if he knew how to bring you back."

His expression twisted at her words.

"I know, Danny," she said. "I know you were sucked through a magic door. You don't have to worry about me not believing."

"It wasn't his fault, Belle. Uncle Lucky warned me not to mess with his stuff when he wasn't there. I was just so sure I knew how to make that spell circle work."

Belle dragged a refurbished armchair close to the bed and sat. She leaned forward over her knees. "So what happened? Where were you all these years?"

Danny pulled one hand down his face. "I was in Faerie, or as I came to call it: The Land of Self-Induced Alzheimer's."

"I don't know what that means."

"Magic is real there, Belle. Like a living, breathing fairytale. It happens on a daily basis, not just now and then like here. The problem is, Faerie isn't stable. Countries go to war over what the rules of magic ought to be, whatever favors the ruling party's particular talents, basically. If the conflict gets too bad, the territory falls into magical anarchy. It's dangerous. Bad things can happen to a lot of people, and since most of them are big mojo faeries, they think they shouldn't have to stub their toes. If a faerie takes a real hurt, like losing a loved one, they tend to erase themselves rather than wait to get over it."

"Erase themselves?"

"They do a spell to take away the memory of the bad thing. Sometimes they erase their whole lives. They feel better, but it tends to make the place chaotic. Let me tell you, the first time you wake up and someone who was your friend suddenly doesn't remember you, it's disconcerting."

"It sounds it," Belle said.

He looked at her, a whole history she hadn't shared shadowing his eyes. Seeing her notice, he shook himself. "I shouldn't complain. Where I ended up was hardly the worst of the territories. People treated me well. I was valuable to them. Because the human world is less changeable, bringing us into their realm helps anchor their reality—once they arrange it the way they like. They were very careful not to erase that knowledge."

"You *were* a prisoner," she breathed. "You didn't make that part up."

Danny rocked his weight back and forth. "I didn't realize it at first. I was having a lot of fun. I was a kid, and I was living out my own sword and sorcery fantasy. When I finally got a clue that they were using me, I felt betrayed, but it was too late. I didn't know how to get back again."

Belle reached out to squeeze his knee. Shoulders bowed, he wagged his head and went on. "The faeries offered to take away my memories more than once. They said I'd feel better if I didn't remember you and home. I couldn't do it. Being me, staying me, seemed like the only thing I could take pride in. I'd been so stupid. I knew how much I must have hurt you. What right did I have not to feel bad?"

"Oh Danny."

Her grown-up little brother wiped fresh tears from his face. "I know. You wouldn't have wanted me to suffer. I made that choice for me."

"I'm glad you did. I'm glad you're still you. And I'm really glad to see you again."

He drew a breath that straightened his spine. Belle decided he was ready for the question that had been bursting to get out since she realized it was him.

"How did you get back here?"

He started to speak, then paused, needing to compose his thoughts. *God*, she prayed, her heart clutching, *I know You've given me a huge blessing here, but please don't let this be bad news.*

"Belle," he finally said, "I know how you are sometimes, but he saved my life more than once. Please don't be mad at him."

"*Him?*" she repeated through her tight throat.

"Your friend Duvall. He came after me through the portal, tracked me halfway across Faerie, and then led me out safely. There are creatures in faerie no human would want to meet alone, and we had to get past them. I know he should have told you why he was leaving before he disappeared, but he thought he was protecting you."

Belle grabbed Danny's arm so tightly she startled him. "He's all right? He isn't dead or hurt?"

This wasn't the reaction Danny was expecting. "Uh," he said. "He's waiting in the car to see if you want to talk to him."

"What car? Here, you mean? Like right outside this house?"

She leaped to her feet, adrenaline causing her heart to feel like it would beat out of her veins. Danny shut his gaping mouth. "He's parked at the bottom of Uncle Lucky's drive. We leased a rental car outside Resurrection. The cars inside the Pocket don't run on human gas."

Belle had no idea what this meant and frankly didn't care. He was here. She had to go to him. She turned in an addled circle, her brain refusing to guide her to her next action.

"I have to go to him," she said.

"Shoes might help," Danny suggested, beginning to look amused. "You can't run through the snow in bare feet."

Her boots were on the rag rug down by the front entry. Rather than run there immediately, she used the last of her concentration to focus on Danny.

"*Thank you*," she said, bending to kiss his cheek. "I'll be back! I'm so happy you made it here!"

"I won't wait up," Danny murmured as she pelted out the door.

CHAPTER 8

D uvall wasn't accustomed to the sort of nervousness that had taken hold of him. Lights off, heater on, he sat in the dark blue car at the foot of the long driveway. The sky was a blanket of darkening gray, the steadily falling snow a reminder of seconds ticking by. He'd parked on the verge of the drive, the wheels edged into a plowed bank under a drooping pine. He was pretty sure he could get the car free again, though part of him wanted to jump out and shovel. Every muscle he had seemed to be overloading with energy.

Calm down, he thought. *What's going to happen is going to happen.*

Even as he told his breathing to slow, he noticed his fingers tapping restlessly on the wheel.

"Fuck," he muttered beneath his breath. He was a prince. He shouldn't be required to exercise self-control. Or maybe if he'd practiced more of it when he was younger, he wouldn't be having trouble now. It chafed that his happiness hung on the acceptance of a mere human.

That was pure faerie arrogance, of course, a trait that wouldn't earn him points with his beloved. Belle was no mere anything. She had her pride the same as him. Her brother was the one who'd learned humility, and he wasn't "mere" either. Duvall liked the young man. They'd gotten to know one another in the course of their escape from anarchic lands. Danny was brave and loyal and a levelheaded swordsman to fight beside. With his sense of humor, he possessed a charm that was almost faerie-like. All in all, given how bitter he had reason to be against the fae, Duvall was proud to have earned his friendship.

Thanks to that friendship, Danny had warned him to brace for Belle tearing multiple strips from his faerie hide. She had a temper, he said, and didn't like to be lied to. Duvall would have to man up and weather the storm.

Duvall thought he could handle that. He simply hoped she'd forgive him once all was said and done. Being apart from her these last few months had deepened his conviction that she was the only woman he wanted to be with.

He swore when he saw his ungloved hands were drumming the wheel again. He gripped it tighter to make them stop. What was Danny doing up at the house? True, he hadn't seen his sister in twenty years, but he knew Duvall was waiting. Maybe Belle had already decided she didn't want to talk to him. Maybe Danny was too kindhearted to break the news.

Duvall hadn't said so, but Danny had figured out he was in love with her.

I can win her back, he thought. *I'm a faerie. I have **skills**. All I need is ten minutes alone with her.*

Duvall groaned. At the thought of being alone her, his cock had stiffened in one long surge. He'd missed her passion so horribly: the sound of her moans when he pleasured her, the heat of her sweet wet sex, the wrap of her arms around him when they were close. Her prickly kindness had won his heart, but her passion had won his body. He couldn't imagine never knowing that again.

If he'd been sure his words wouldn't come to pass, he'd have cursed Danny for making him swear a solemn oath against using magic to woo her.

Calm, he repeated, realizing his hands were nearly snapping the wheel in two. Mundane world or no, he was stronger than humans. He glanced at the dashboard clock. Barely half an hour had passed since Danny left the car. Danny might need more time than that for his explanations. Duvall wondered if he should have let Belle's brother return to Kingaken on his own. He could have prepared the ground. Given Belle a chance to cool down. Duvall's cousins had wanted him to spend the holidays in Resurrection. Though supportive, like his parents they didn't really get that every molecule of his being was tugging him elsewhere.

Belle, he prayed. *Please don't harden your heart to me.*

His heart jumped into his throat as he spied a shape approaching quickly down the snow-whitened drive.

He was out of the car in seconds, running up the rutted slope. Belle was in a long red coat, the color of the wool so vibrant it burned against the snow even in twilight. She hadn't stopped to button the front. The edges flapped around her willow-wand figure, exposing what seemed to be the same crazy-making black silk dress she'd had on the night he arrived. Her boots came nearly to her knees, but her thighs were completely bare.

Duvall didn't have words for how sexy this was to him.

"Duvall!" she cried.

He sped ahead and caught her.

She was freezing, shivering in his arms as he pulled her inside the open edges of his puffed-up down coat. He was glad then that his cousins had bullied him into buying it. He'd wear a thousand silly garments to warm his love. A stab of strangely joyous pain drove upward from his groin. He was holding her, his Belle, his beautiful other half.

Just in case her cry hadn't been a welcome, he crashed his mouth on hers. If this was his last chance to kiss her, he didn't want to miss out.

He guessed it wasn't his last chance. She drove her arms underneath his jacket and attacked his tongue with hers.

Duvall didn't know how to be polite. He had to touch her. Without preamble or permission, he shoved his hand between her trembling legs, under the short silk dress. She made a sound: a groan, a plea—he wasn't about to release her mouth to discover which. He shifted his hand instead, sliding two fingers under her panties and into her. The rest of her might be chilled, but inside her was a pool of incredible liquid heat. Duvall moaned, an agony of lust spiking at the feel of it. If she didn't come in the next ten seconds, *he* was going to scream.

"Mmm," she groaned into his kiss as he worked the hard caress in and out. Her sheath began to flutter, her neck starting to arch back.

Before he could send her over, she wrenched her mouth free of his. "I want *you*, Duvall. I want your cock where your fingers are."

Her words stalled his brain. She fought to open his jeans' tight zipper, his erection pushing against the teeth too hard to easily drag them down. It didn't help that every drop of his former nervous energy had converted to desire.

"Okay," he gasped, pulling wet fingers free of her. "I'll get it."

The rasp of the zipper was music to both their ears. Belle grabbed his collar and kissed him, pulling him with her, over her, as she dropped onto snowy ground. The breath *oomphed* out of him when they hit.

"The car—"

"No," she said, sucking the lobe of his ear so that the hair on his scalp prickled.

"But it's warm. I had the heater on."

"No." She drove her hand down into his briefs, her fingers fiery on the sensitive engorged pole. His body responded helplessly, a gush of pre-ejaculate slicking up her wrist. Belle smoothed it up and down him with far too much enthusiasm for his unraveling self-control.

"I'm warm," she cooed, stroking him all over as his brains melted with pleasure. "I'm warmer than anything."

To prove it, her legs split around him, the flimsy dress riding up, the firmness of her thighs hugging him. Too breathless to curse, Duvall shoved his jeans down his hips with half-crazed eagerness.

The needs of his libido were shorting out his good sense. Here was fine. Here was great. Her crimson coat was plenty of protection between them and the cold ground. Hardly caring if this was true, he ripped her panties violently free of her, shifting his hips toward hers almost before the scraps of lace were gone. Her thumb and forefinger ringed his shaft, pulling him more precisely into place. There could be no doubt where she wanted him. His crest kissed her sultry heat, the knob gliding perfectly to the opening that awaited it.

An emotion too primitive for a name gripped him. Nothing could stop him from claiming her.

"*Yes*," he said and drove inward in one fell stroke.

The world momentarily stopped turning. Their lips had come together again, as if—instinctively—they wanted to be joined everywhere. Belle's mouth curved in a smile under his. Duvall let out a purring sound. His cock throbbed inside her—hard, hot, fully engulfed in its favorite home. Belle's palms made a soothing pass over the back of his shirt. Her touch felt so good, he had to try to wriggle deeper into her.

"Better?" he murmured, unable to keep his own smile inside.

"Yes," she said, opening dreamy eyes. "You could fuck me now. Really hard, if you don't mind."

He rubbed their noses together, thinking her suggestion sounded a bit too good. "You wouldn't rather we made love?"

"Later," she said, never guessing how this one word made his soul thrum with joy. "Anyway, it's always making love with you."

He'd wanted to take his time, or at least not savage her like Priapus. His long-denied hormones had their own agenda. The slow stroke he meant to savor somehow turned into two desperate thrusts, then four, then a dozen and then they were slamming each other as if neither had a lick of judgment in their heads.

"God," he growled, gripping her hips so he could yank her up him harder.

"More," she said, her head thrashing in the snow.

Her boot heels dug into his rear when she climaxed that first time.

"Ah," he cried, his head jerking back as she clamped on him. His own orgasm rose from his tailbone. He wanted to hold on, but he just couldn't. She was going so hard.

And moaning. And creaming all over him. The ball of fire in him exploded, rushing up his cock in a great hot rush.

He came like he was emptying out his soul, the glow of relief so strong it was a turn on.

Belle's dark green eyes were even dreamier then. Her nails scratched lightly along his back underneath his shirt. She was touching his bare skin, which he'd been dreaming of her doing ever since he left. Duvall's balls tried to quiver with pleasure.

"Again?" she asked.

He was still moving inside her. Not as hard, because he knew he'd really gone at her, but truthfully he couldn't stop. He'd only softened a bit, and the sleek wet friction of her pussy was a drug to his cock, one he'd been missing terribly.

He cleared his throat before he answered. "Are you asking because you've had enough, or because you're wondering if I'm capable?"

"Oh I can tell you're capable," she laughed throatily. "That *again* was meant to be a request."

"Oh," he said, the skin of his cock abruptly tight as a drum again.

Belle rocked her pelvis up him, twisting it in an extremely interesting fashion. Rockets of sensation shot up his sexual nerves.

"*Again*," she teased, without the question mark.

She shouldn't have got to him the way she did, not when he'd just come like a dam bursting.

"I love you," he said, wanting her to hear that before he got caught up again.

"I love you too," she said back.

He lost control, utterly and completely, as if one expression of care from her held the power of the entire fae nation.

"God," he said, plunging back into her full length.

Her hands gripped his butt, and they were off again. This bout was no more elegant than the first, though they did get their rhythms better coordinated. They both enjoyed that, groaning out their pleasure as the hard, long thrusts increased speed in synchrony. It was as if their bodies shared a single intelligence, and their minds couldn't interfere. Duvall suspected there were monsters who couldn't hump this hard. His cock was practically singing an aria to ecstasy.

Belle improved matters further by digging her boot heels into the ground.

"Fuck, I missed this," he panted as her fingernails pricked his back muscles. When her pussy tightened, he couldn't help grunting in approval.

He was going to go any second, and God help her, so was she.

"Don't . . . make me scream," she gasped.

He immediately churned his hips twice as fast.

She did scream, at least for a few seconds. Duvall might have shouted a bit himself. Gratified to his bones, he slung in deep and poured himself into her. Lord, it felt good: his cock, her pussy, all that wetness and heat surrounding him as he came and came. As his second killer ejaculation tapered, a delicious slow-motion tingle rolled up his spine.

That had been a release for the record books.

"Idiot," she said, smacking his shoulder without much anger. "I have people up at the house."

Duvall panted a couple times. "I doubt they heard. Besides which, didn't I offer to take you in the car?"

"Take me there now," she said.

Duvall rose on his elbows, his energy recovering magically. His eyes were warm enough that they must have been close to glowing.

"Please?" she added, smiling coyly. "I'd really like to get more clothes off you."

"Whatever my beloved wishes," was all he could think to say.

~

Now that her most urgent hungers were satisfied, Belle wasn't letting either of them off with another quickie. They groaned at having to move, but the car *was* warm, and Duvall was too pretty a present not to unwrap a bit. With that in mind, she pushed him ahead of her into the back seat.

"Have I mentioned I like women who know what they want?" he said.

She laughed, suspecting what most would want was anything at all from him. "This must be your lucky day then," she said aloud.

Straddling him, she pulled off her coat, then unbuttoned and removed his shirt. This was a lovely garment in navy silk. Seeing it made her realize she'd only ever seen him dressed as John Feeney. Though casual, his jeans fit like they'd been tailored, and the denim was butter soft. She wondered if being a faerie prince meant he could afford bespoke clothes, then decided she didn't care. He was here, and her hands were on him. That was what mattered.

Rubbing her hands up his jean-clad thighs, feeling how firm those long muscles were, was the simplest of dreams come true. His cock stirred where the cloth lay open. Duvall had known better than to re-zip; his needs were as difficult to exhaust as hers. For a moment, Belle admired the way his seed shone on the stiffening organ.

Clearly Duvall was recovering his aplomb. He stacked his hands behind his head, deliberately drawing her attention to his finely-honed torso. She noticed the scar he'd once had was gone. Though she missed it a little, Belle didn't think she'd ever seen a male animal so gorgeous.

"Are you going to ogle me all night?" he asked.

His eyes had taken on the gleam she knew was part of his faerie nature, little fires smoldering in the depths of his pupils. She combed her fingers up the sheer dark hair on his chest, like ruffling a cat backwards. His skin was warm and lay close to his muscles, his nipples tightened to red points. She relished knowing he was excited too—possibly more than he was letting on.

"I had more than ogling in mind," she said, reversing her stroke and circling his navel. "But perhaps I should let you choose. Do you have a special request?"

He licked his lips. "Anything is good. I missed everything about you."

This was nice, but men didn't mean *anything* when they licked their lips like that. He confirmed her theory by tightening his glutes, which lifted his pelvis a suggestive bit. His legs were too long to fit the width of the car. To compensate, his left foot was on the seat and his right planted on the floor. This gave his thighs the perfect spread for her purposes.

"Scoot closer to the door," she said, waving him back toward it.

He wedged his shoulders into the space she indicated, his eyes never leaving her.

She was sure his gaze remained on her as she bent to him. He'd guessed where this was headed, and he was going to watch. His cock was almost as hard as it got when she sucked it into her mouth.

Pulling her lips snugly to the rim and flicking finished the job nicely.

"Belle," he sighed, the sound as sweet as the feel of his steely rod.

She pushed halfway down and drew up again. "You taste like Christmas," she said.

He cupped her cheek tenderly. "Do you *want* to do this for me, sweetheart? I can't help enjoying everything better if you enjoy it too."

She'd noticed her arousal gave him a charge, but he seemed to mean this literally. "Really? You can't help it?"

"Human desire is a kind of drug for the fae. Because I love you, yours is almost impossible for me to resist."

"Wow." She swallowed, her spine gone hot. That was a trait with possibilities. "I guess I don't mind admitting one taste of you makes me not want to stop."

His eyes seemed to shoot real fire at her.

"Don't stop then, please," he rasped.

She didn't stop after that. She went down on his silken cock until his big body trembled and his hands forked into her hair. His breath came in shaky gasps she wanted to memorize. Her own body burned, but she loved playing with him this way.

His enjoyment was her drug too.

His balls drew up for her gentle squeezes, warm and tight in her palms. She slid her hands up his torso to pinch his contracted nipples, and he writhed wonderfully for her. His scent rose as he began to sweat, making her head spin and her pussy ache with desire. She wanted him in her, but even more she wanted him to know he was loved.

With a hum of unadulterated pleasure, she ducked down farther to lap his testicles, pushing them closer to his body with the flat of her tongue. Though he widened his sprawl to give her more access, he also groaned like this was too much. Belle moved the wet firm drag to his underridge, increasing the pressure as she licked across the sweet spot beneath his flare.

That bundle of erotic nerves was worth spending more than one minute on.

When he let out what sounded suspiciously like a whimper, she sucked him into her mouth again.

He must have missed her surrounding him. "Belle," he gasped, his thigh muscles bunching with pleasure and tension. "*God.*"

Despite his obvious excitement, he didn't ask her to stop. She had a feeling he didn't want to come in her mouth, but he seemed determined to savor every second of her gift short of that. Appreciating that and wanting to give him all she could, she held him still on her tongue. She didn't bob up and down, but kept her lips closed around him, her cheeks pulling and releasing soft and wet on his shaft.

Apparently, this was a nice sensation.

"Belle," he said, rough with wonder as he alternately squirmed and fought to stay motionless. The idea that she was the first to do this to him was heady. The taste of spice increased in her mouth, his faerie pre-cum leaking more quickly from his slit. "*Belle.*"

His hands fisted in her hair, his hips jerking up—involuntarily, she thought. She guessed she'd finally reached his limit. She eased up him, gently, dropping one last kiss to his quivering tip. To her surprise, when she sat back, a cloud of dancing rainbow sparkles filled the interior of the car.

Duvall smiled as her eyes widened at the sight.

"So," he said huskily, "now you know what happens when you arouse a faerie past the point of reining in his magic."

"It's pretty," she marveled.

"Not as pretty as you," he returned.

She wrinkled her nose, and he shook his head. Faeries couldn't lie, she remembered. Perhaps she had to believe that, to him, she was attractive. Still smiling, he slid his hands around her snow-dampened hair, down her back, and onto her butt. It wasn't much of a journey from gliding over the short silk dress to sliding under it. Belle shivered as his beautiful fingers probed forward.

"Now we make love," he said.

He didn't seem to mean right away. He hitched her closer to his front, continuing to play his touch over her drenched labia. His longest finger brushed her clitoris, tracing its swollen shape so gently her spine shivered.

"Need an intermission to recover your self-control?" Belle had meant to sound teasing; he *was* a faerie with an extra sexual gift or two, after all. Despite her intent, the question came out breathless.

"Maybe," he admitted, his mouth slanting humorously.

Without warning, a spark shot from his finger and up her clit. Belle shrieked, jumped, and Duvall burst out laughing.

"Sorry," he said, not looking it at all. "Couldn't resist. I didn't hurt you, did I?"

The shock had been a teeny lightning bolt blazing up her nerves. It had left her more aroused than before—no accident, she was sure. "You know you didn't," she told him narrowly.

He moved his hands onto seemingly safer ground, smoothing behind her thighs. "I like your boots," he observed. "Do you suppose I could peel off this dress? I'd like it if you weren't wearing anything but them."

"If I agree, will you get on with it?"

He laughed, low and male. "I expect I will," he said.

Two tall people in a compact four-door didn't make undressing easy, but with her cooperation, Duvall stripped off the dress without ripping it. Belle wasn't a hundred percent comfortable being this bare a stone's throw from a public road. Duvall drove that from her mind the second he slid his palms up her front. He covered her slight breasts completely, the kneading of his fingers causing her to wriggle with pleasure. He hadn't forgotten how sensitive she was there.

"That's better," he said, a deliberate noblesse oblige in his tone. "You could take me now, if you like."

She did like, enough let him off the hook for teasing her.

She positioned him with a pleasure she didn't try to hide, sinking slowly onto that hot thickness. She was so wet and relaxed her body gave way for him like a dream.

The charm of that definitely hadn't worn off.

"Mmm," he said, nuzzling up the side of her neck. "Belle, you're my paradise."

He was hers. Too lost in pleasure and need to speak, she tried to prove it with her body. He helped her ride him, his hands steadying her hips. His fingers stretched onto her bottom like he couldn't bear not to caress it. The most delicious tension built between them. They'd shared releases already, but both of them wanted more. In an endearing show of vulnerability, especially considering his nature, his teeth caught his lower lip. Like her, he thought what was between them was almost too good to stand.

Belle licked the lip he was biting. Duvall pulled her closer yet, their naked fronts rubbing together as they rocked up and down. He kissed her—once, deeply—then had to break off to breathe. His head arched back, his arm muscles tightening. The tiniest tremor started in his thighs.

His cock went very, *very* hard inside her.

"I want to keep you," she whispered, unable to restrain the words. "I know maybe I can't, but if I could, I would."

His eyes had been closed, their lids tensed by exquisite sensations. They opened at her confession. His pupils were huge, his expression glazed with desire.

"Marry me, Belle," he said.

She missed her stroke. Duvall slid his hands to her waist and rubbed.

"Marry me," he said again.

"If you say it three times, will I have to?" she blurted.

He smiled and—oh—his dark eyes said he knew her right to the core: her weaknesses, her strengths, the quirks that would have bugged the heck out of other men. "I promised your brother I wouldn't magick you."

"Then yes," she said. "I'd be happy to marry you."

His gorgeous face split into a brilliant grin. "Good," he said, his hips pushing with sudden breath-stealing assertiveness into her. "We'll settle all the details once I've made you come again."

The idea of details gave her pause. Had she just promised something she shouldn't have? Duvall had no trouble reading her expression.

"Uh-uh," he warned, his hips shocking hard into her again. It couldn't be chance that his smooth round glans pummeled her sweet spot. "No second thoughts, Miss Hobart. You are going to let me make you happy."

She guessed she was. She sucked air in sharply as his killingly accurate strokes quickened.

"Oh God," she gasped.

She couldn't go fast enough to keep up with him. His talk of *making* her come might sound arrogant, but he easily demonstrated that it was not. His arms clamped around her, moving her, controlling her with a show of strength he must have known would drive her crazy. Kinks she couldn't switch off flipped to the stuck-in-"on" position. She grew wetter, wilder, a tornado in his arms.

"Shit," he breathed, but not like he minded.

He slammed his cock into her, driving her right to the edge of climax. He hadn't lied about her desires heightening his. Everything she felt—which was *plenty*—was affecting him. He was harder, thicker, each pump into her more desperate. He grunted with his efforts to give her more, his beautiful face distorting as he tried to hold on through it. Her orgasm shimmered, built. She pulled tighter on his erection, drawing a gasp from him.

Her sheath fisted hard as her nerves finally went haywire. She had just enough self-possession to rub the special spot on his shoulder blades where his wings would have extended.

"Augh," Duvall cried, jamming his cock as deeply as it would go. "*Belle!*"

Her name rose into a scream. Heat flooded out from him into her—not just from his cock, but all his energy searing her. Belle rolled into another tidal wave climax, her body shuddering with it. Sharp little pleasure shocks ricocheted through her sex, as if his come were charged with electricity.

Duvall must have felt the effect as well. He twitched and groaned, his cock jerking wildly within her, seemingly beyond his control.

"Jeez," he sighed, settling at last beneath her.

Belle grinned smugly. Her cheek rested on his shoulder, which was the perfect support for it. Faerie or not, he was sweating like a horse.

She was never going to forget that she'd made him scream.

"I guess that doesn't happen all the time," she mumbled into his neck. "Even to faeries."

Duvall snorted, his hand sliding warmly but also somewhat tiredly around her rear. "If you're fishing for compliments, my beloved, I'll happily give you all you want."

~

Leaving the car right away wasn't an option. They were too disheveled and sweaty to expose themselves to Belle's company. Well, Belle was. Duvall didn't seem self-conscious about that sort of thing.

He'd pulled her against him, arms loosely wrapping her body as her back rested on his front. Belle's skin still vibrated with her quickened pulse, but she felt peaceful. She rubbed his forearms, then dragged her coat from where it hung over the front seat and used it to cover them. If her guests happened to drive back this way, she wasn't going to be caught in her birthday suit.

"I'm glad you're not mad at me," Duvall said sleepily.

"I should be," she retorted. "Why didn't you tell me you were rescuing Danny?"

"I didn't want to get your hopes up. I wasn't sure I could find him . . . or return myself. I thought enough people in your life had disappointed you."

"And you thought me feeling abandoned would be better?"

"You didn't feel abandoned," he said.

She didn't realize this was true until he said it. She'd had other reactions but not that. "You closed the door behind you," she said. "You made certain I couldn't follow you."

"I closed *a* door," he corrected, "not every door to your world. And, yes, I made certain you couldn't follow. I flattered myself that you'd try, and you could have ended up anywhere. Unless inter-dimensional portals are anchored expertly—which this one was not—they don't lead predictably from point A to point B. What would you have done if you'd ended up in a hell dimension? More importantly, what would *I*?"

"Spoken like a prince," she said with a choking laugh.

"Well, I am one," he said, his dignity aggrieved. "What I meant, however, was that I'd have *had* to come after you, which might not have ended well for either of us. You might not realize this, and I don't mean to suggest I'm not willing, but I'm giving up quite a bit to marry you and live here."

She twisted around in his arms to look up at him.

"I'm *more* than willing," he clarified, his expression softening.

"Will you miss your power?" she asked, because perhaps his comment hadn't been as self-centered as she'd thought.

"I'll have some," he said, affecting a shrug that didn't entirely convince. "My power will simply restore itself more slowly. And I'll still have my faerie luck. We'll have a nice life here."

"Would you want to bring me to Faerie?"

"Absolutely not," he said unequivocally. "You can meet my parents in Resurrection. It's a half-and-half city, magic-wise, much more stable than Faerie and much less dangerous for humans. You'll like it, I believe. My faerie cousins think anyone who lives in the Old Country is crazy."

Belle touched his chest, trying to understand the sentiment behind his acerbic words. "Are your parents going to be upset with you for wanting to marry me?"

"Worried maybe, but not upset. They love me. My happiness always matters most to them." He said this simply, but also as if he knew how special it was. "My family is the main reason I love Faerie. Under their rule, Talfryn is wonderful."

"Love makes any place a home."

"That has been my experience," he said.

He regarded her so warmly she was humbled. "Are you sure?" she asked. "You really want to marry me?"

"I do," he confirmed. "I believe you're the other half of me."

"So . . . like it or not, you're stuck is what you're saying?"

He laughed and kissed the tip of her nose. "I don't think of it as stuck, Tinker Belle. I think of it as lucky."

Belle thought of it as lucky too. She put her head on his shoulder, and he rested his chin on top. "Danny *would* tell you that stupid nickname."

"You have to admit it's appropriate. Plus, every faerie bride can use a few extra names."

"Like you have my uncle's now."

"Like I have your uncle's. If you wish, you could choose a last name for me to use every day."

"I'll think on that," she said, too lazy to move away from the strong beating of his heart.

"Nothing too ridiculous," he cautioned. "You'll have to share it soon enough."

Oh, he had a thing or two to learn about women in her world—though maybe not on that particular score. "I'm not fragile," she did feel compelled to say. "I'm strong enough to face hard things. My ex used to call me tough-as-nails Belle."

Duvall hummed and stroked her hair. He seemed to have an opinion about the nickname but kept it to himself. "I wouldn't want you any other way," he said.

More than him being a faerie made Belle believe this.

~

Duvall hugged his betrothed in the warm dark car surrounded by winter cold. As he did, he experienced a peace so profound it could only be a gift from the Power his kind didn't contemplate as often as humans did. Faeries were demigods themselves: dimension creators, when it suited them. They knew, though, that greater hands than theirs had formed the universe.

Duvall listened to snowflakes tick on the frosted glass, perfectly happy that this was so.

Belle didn't understand what he gave up for her. Later she might, and he anticipated a few arguments. If he remained in Faerie, he'd exist for centuries. With Belle, in the mundane world, he'd have one long lifetime. When she was ready to cross the veil as her uncle had, Duvall would cross with her. He had more evidence than most humans that they wouldn't cease to be, but even if he hadn't, his decision would be the same.

Time without meaning was only time. Whatever came, he knew he'd never erase a moment he spent with her. With a sureness that ran deeper than instinct, he knew his life here with her, in the place she considered home, was the meaning his many years had been leading to.

Belle was the sparkling spirit that inspired his to its best shine.

His hands tingled as he stroked her love-tangled hair, encouraging her to cuddle closer under the scarlet coat. Sleep had almost claimed him when a snatch of a vision rose into his mind's eye. Future-telling wasn't his strongest ability, but now and then it nudged him.

"A treasure shop," he said.

"Hm?" Belle hummed into his chest muscle.

"We're going to run one together," he predicted, "full of things your kind have discarded that other humans still desire. Also, there will be pie. We're going to call it Ring My Belle's."

"Oh God," Belle groaned.

Duvall smiled. He knew he had spoken true.

EPILOGUE

B elle and Duvall were married on New Year's Day, a decision everyone—with the exception of Danny and Mrs. J—considered hasty.

In Susi's case, this might have been because she'd wanted to plan a big wedding.

They honeymooned in Resurrection, which Belle actually did think was a mistake. The half-magic Pocket city was far too fascinating to permit them (or her, at any rate) to spend the whole week in bed. Plus, Duvall's family arrived three nights later to throw them a big dinner. His father and mother (the king and queen!) were very nice but a teensy bit intimidating. Belle didn't meet Duvall's two older brothers, because they'd stayed behind to govern Talfryn.

Duvall's famously fierce big sisters only popped in to eat. Somewhat to the other faeries' shock, they'd sworn vengeance upon Mor, Duvall's name-stealing enemy. Effie and Mina, who were twins, had shared a dream in which they cut him down together with iron swords, and they'd taken this as a sign that their special sisterly bond would give them the power required. Since the word from the soothsayers was also favorable, everyone pretended not to worry for their safety.

Belle was learning life in the "Old Country" wasn't what she was used to.

Duvall's Resurrection cousins turned out to be a raucous bunch once they had some OJ in them. Danny especially hit it off with them. He'd spent so many years in Faerie, she supposed he might now miss that. As generous as they were fun, the cousins gave her and Duvall some pretty awesome wedding presents, most of which he warned her wouldn't work in the mundane world. Belle didn't care about that. Lucky dragon teeth and good wishes for heart-held friends were way more thoughtful than waffle irons.

One more advantage of their visit to Resurrection was that Duvall's wings were real there. They were almost lovelier than she could comprehend. Their iridescence was exquisite, their colors and their sparkles, the way they glowed like the northern lights with his emotions. Duvall explained that displaying them was a private thing. *They* were his nakedness. Despite their beauty, his wings were unexpectedly tough for organs so expressive and sensitive: the strongest part of him, he claimed.

The fun Belle had exploring them meant their honeymoon went over by a few days.

When they returned to Kingaken, tired but happy, she and Danny bit the bullet on apprising their parents—in an edited fashion—of the latest developments. Even though Danny remembered what they were like, he was taken aback by their wild joy over his reappearance . . . and their utter indifference to Belle's marriage. Because he felt he had to, he went to visit them briefly in New Mexico. He was very quiet for a couple days afterwards. When he did speak of the trip, all he said was that he was never seeing them in person again.

He lived with Belle and Duvall for six months—decompressing from his time in Faerie, as he put it. When asked if he'd prefer relocating to Resurrection, he shook his head. "Here is better, Belle. Here is steady and good. Even in Resurrection there's too much magic for me to relax." Hearing how adamant he was allowed Belle to relax herself. He wasn't staying in Kingaken just for her. Despite the unavoidable bumped elbows, the time spent as roomies was healing for both siblings.

Danny paid his keep by pitching in at their new junkshop. Kingaken's economy had taken a small but decided upswing, a mysterious turn of events if you hadn't learned firsthand how faerie "luck" could spread. She knew Duvall enjoyed playing a part in that. Watching him and Mrs. J work their magic at estate sales was an education in the one-two punch created when human bargaining know-how joined forces with faerie charm.

Organizing the business and restoring stock was left to Belle, which suited her to her toes. She'd happily have gone on as they were forever, but one morning over breakfast, Danny announced he was ready to stand on his own. He'd bought a decrepit Victorian mansion on the far side of town, which he and the Feeneys were going to fix up. He planned to turn it into a bed and breakfast for Kingaken's now steady stream of antiquers.

Belle had grown fond of having him underfoot, but since the other side of town was barely two miles away, she couldn't be too upset.

By the time the B&B was open, Duvall's sisters had successfully accomplished their quest to kill Mor. Defeating the ancient evildoer had made them such celebrities they'd felt a need to flee the magic world until the hubbub died down. They were Danny's first guests, their faerie glamour ensuring the place would smell heavenly for years.

On a more practical note, Belle decided to call her husband Duvall Duvall, because it made her laugh every time she heard it, and because him having only one everyday moniker gave that name the least possible power over him.

He claimed she'd chosen it in revenge for him insisting they call their thriving junkshop his predicted Ring My Belle's.

"That was for luck," he liked to complain. "Because I saw it. Calling me Duvall Duvall was uncalled for."

Belle didn't buy his pretense of being upset. Her handsome prince of a husband was a treasure worth protecting, brightening the power he'd been born to with simpler magic of being a good man.

Since he felt the same about treasuring her, that worked out perfectly.

◆ ◆ ◆

Want to read what happens next for Duvall and Belle?
Check out the first chapter for *The Faerie's Honeymoon*!

THE FAERIE'S HONEYMOON:
CHAPTER 1

T he faerie prince known as Duvall Duvall—very much not his truename, thank you—was bringing his human bride to the world of magic for the first time.

The trip was their honeymoon, their destination the half-magic city of Resurrection in upstate New York. Invisible to most humans, Resurrection was what was known as a "Pocket" city. A number of these had been created by Duvall's brethren, places where humans and other races could interact to the hopeful benefit of both. As long as the race could play nice with others, the fae granted it visas. Today, Resurrection sheltered shapeshifters, demons, humans with "extra" talents, and quite a number of other beings. The original land of Faerie, whose essence had gone into forming the Pockets, was too often a magical Wild West: lawless, chaotic, and more than even some fae could handle.

Duvall could handle quite a lot. He'd spent the majority of his life in Faerie. His parents ruled the land of Talfryn with a steadier hand than most. If an enemy hadn't chased him into the human realm, where he'd had the supreme good fortune of meeting his future wife, Duvall expected he'd still reside in the Old Country.

His wife had changed everything, Fate bless her.

At the current moment, his beloved was trying unsuccessfully to wave down a train station porter to help them with their luggage.

"Belle," he said, gently rubbing the sleeve of her beautiful red wool coat. The suburban platform was open to the winter weather, and—unlike him—she needed the garment for warmth.

"They're ignoring me," she said, craning around the other departing passengers. There were more than usual. Humans rarely noticed the Resurrection stop existed. Magic protected it from ordinary sight. Duvall expected the Weretiger New Year celebrations explained the crowd. Any supes who'd scattered beyond the borders would return home for Resurrection's weeklong version of Mardi Gras. Unfortunately for Belle, this meant she had to compete with beings who more naturally drew the station staff's attention.

She clucked in annoyance as yet another porter rushed to serve someone else. "This is worse than trying to hail a taxi in Manhattan. I knew I shouldn't have packed everything I own. Now we'll be stuck lugging the stuff ourselves. How did you get away with just an overnight case?"

Duvall got away with an overnight case because, here in Resurrection, he could magick anything he wanted. Already, he could feel his batteries sucking up ambient power. They hadn't been able to do that while he was in her world. Now they filled so quickly he was getting a head rush.

"Belle," he said more firmly, giving her lovely straight hair a tug.

"What?" she said, a hint of a snap in it. A second later, remorse pinched her mouth.

He smiled. Belle sometimes felt guilty for her temper, but he knew the passionate heart it was an outgrowth of. "They can't see you, sweetheart. As a . . . non-magical human, you're nearly invisible to them."

"Really?" Belle said, her annoyance fading as her curiosity rose.

"Really. I know it's inconvenient, but it prevents humans who don't have an invitation into the Pocket from being accidentally escorted in."

She peered back at the uniformed porters, most of whom were elves or mixbloods—though that wouldn't be obvious to her. More spells hid traits like pointy ears or oddly colored skin. Observing nothing peculiar, she returned her gaze to him. At the sight of her dear pretty face, his heart turned over. God, he loved her, from her mysterious dark green eyes to her long straight nose to her wonderful willow-wand figure. Belle's parents hadn't exactly built up her self esteem, as humans liked to say on talk shows. His darling didn't always think of herself as attractive, but she'd become the image of love to him.

Her lips curved as she recognized his expression. "You're going gooey again."

"Faeries don't go gooey," he said, mostly to see her grin.

She didn't disappoint, her teeth flashing with the acerbic humor he loved. "Careful, Mr. Duvall. That's sailing very close to a lie. I wouldn't want you giving yourself a headache before we reach the hotel."

"Certainly not before I summon a porter."

"Can you?" she asked.

Duvall smiled and let his concealing glamour fall.

Duvall's powers had been substantially curtailed in her realm. Belle had seen him twinkle in shared dreams and in heightened moments of lovemaking. Like all fae, he was out-of-the-ordinary good looking in any reality, enough that he'd thought it best to cover up on the train. As a result, this was Belle's first glimpse of him fully charged and in his element. While Duvall couldn't deny he'd been looking forward to showing off for his beloved, he wasn't prepared for how taken aback she was.

"Wow," she said a little shakily. "With a heaping helping of gosh."

Duvall's stomach went oddly tight. Had he frightened her? Would his alien display cause her to regard him in a less easy light? He didn't want that. Many races liked to claim faeries were half pride, but Belle was his equal in every way that counted. In truth, Belle was his soul mate.

Before he could decide what to say to make it better, a bowing elf porter rushed over. To go by the gold braid on his uniform, he was the captain of the station's crew.

"Prince Duvall, sir!" he exclaimed. "Forgive me for not seeing you there. How may I serve you and your companion?"

Elves sometimes resented faeries, who—admittedly—didn't let them forget they were a few rungs down on the magical power scale. Duvall gave this one points for referring to Belle politely. Elves were much less snobbish than faeries, but even they occasionally snubbed non-magical humans.

"No matter, cousin," he said, for that's what elves were to faeries. "We'd like our luggage organized and a limo to transport us to the Downtown Grande. Also, if you could recommend a trustworthy driver, I'd be grateful. This is my wife's first visit to the city. We'll probably do some sightseeing."

The elf's slanty brows went up a millimeter at him identifying Belle as his wife.

Faeries dallied with humans considerably more than they married them.

"I believe we can satisfy you, sir," he said. "There's a brand-new Spink demon come on staff. Passed the gargoyles' trust test with flying colors. Darius knows the city and can make sure you and your wife aren't bothered by riffraff, no matter where you go."

Duvall hesitated. Trust test notwithstanding, he wasn't sure he wanted to expose Belle to a demon so early on. He hadn't forgotten her ear-splitting scream of reaction to her first ghost.

"It is Weretiger New Year," the elf reminded. "Hard to rent muscle at the last minute."

This was true. He looked at Belle, whose eyes were as round as saucers. He'd explained to her that some demons lived here, but it wasn't the same as being driven around by one. "Would you like that? It'll be safe enough. The gargoyles' psychic exams are difficult to jigger. Plus, you'd want someone with you if you did any wandering on your own."

"I'd like to meet a demon," she said. "I'm just afraid I'll accidentally do something insensitive. Will it be offended if I say 'Oh God'?"

The elf burst into a surprised laugh, which he then attempted to cover with a cough.

Duvall searched for a diplomatic way to explain the porter's amusement, one that wouldn't reflect too badly on his own kind. He'd known Belle long enough to guess at her ideas of what was fair. "Demons have very strict visas, my beloved, and faeries more or less set the rules for them staying here."

"You mean the demon wouldn't dare complain, no matter what I did."

"Yes," Duvall admitted with a sigh. "But it's also probably very grateful to be here instead of its former home. They don't call them hell dimensions for nothing. It truly might not feel an insult, given that."

"Spinks aren't religious," the elf added, "if sir will pardon my saying so. You can swear to anything you want in front of them. Just be yourself, ma'am. They've met enough mundanes to know how you folks are."

His unthinking use of the pejorative made Belle bite her lip in amusement. Mundane wasn't the most PC term for non-magical humans. Aware he'd used it once or twice himself, Duvall decided not to kick up a fuss.

"All right," his beloved said to the elf. "We appreciate your help."

* * *

About the Author

Emma Holly is the award winning, *USA Today* bestselling author of more than forty romantic books featuring billionaires, genies, faeries and just plain extraordinary folks. She loves the hot stuff, both to read and to write!

If you'd like to discover what else she's written, please visit her website at www.emmaholly.com.

Emma runs monthly contests and sends out newsletters that often include notice of special sales. To receive them, go to her contest page.

Thanks so much for reading this book. If you enjoyed it, please consider leaving a review. That kind of support is very helpful!

Three full-length paranormal romances: *Hidden Talents, Hidden Depths* and *Hidden Crimes*. Whether they're irresistible werewolf cops, sexy wereseal kings, or sassy firefighting tigresses, these supernatural heroes turn up the heat!

Books 1 – 3 in the Hidden Series

"The perfect package of supes, romance, mystery and HEA!"
—**Paperback Dolls** on *Hidden Talents*

"You will fall head over heels [with] the amazingly sensuous and intensely graphic world . . . One of the best erotic romances I have ever read."
—**BittenByLove** on *Hidden Depths*

"If you are looking for suspense, passion and a touch of the paranormal, don't look any farther than *Hidden Crimes*."—**Joyfully Reviewed**

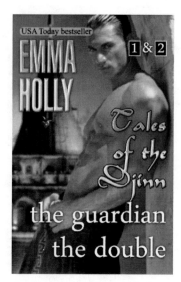

When a mysterious stranger with a briefcase full of cash moves into Elyse's brownstone, she never imagines he's a genie. Cade is gorgeous and sophisticated, but nothing about him adds up . . . that is, until she learns he's a magical being desperate to break a curse on his home city.

Teaming up with a human female isn't the only challenge Elyse's tenant will have to face. His trip to Elyse's world created a duplicate of himself, a not-quite carbon copy who believes *he's* Cade's superior.

Commander Arcadius should be easy for Elyse to resist. He's arrogant, insensitive, and a chauvinist—making it obvious he doesn't think much of her. Then, bit-by-bit, she sees past his prickly exterior. Arcadius is who Cade used to be before they met. If she fell for one man, chances are she'll fall for the other.

Two full-length novels of the Djinn

"FANTASTIC! [T]his may be the best thing she has written to date . . . an epic tale of romantic fantasy."—**In My Humble Opinion**

"Addictive . . . should not be missed!"—**Long and Short Reviews**

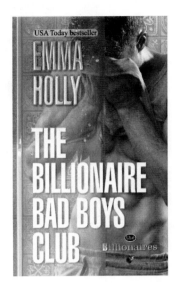

Self-made billionaires Zane and Trey have been a club of two since they were eighteen. They've done everything together: play football, fall in love, even get smacked around by their dads. The only thing they haven't tried is seducing the same woman. When they set their sights on sexy chef Rebecca, these bad boys meet their match!

"This book is a mesmerizing, beautiful and oh-my-gods-hot work of art!"
—**BittenByLove** 5-hearts review

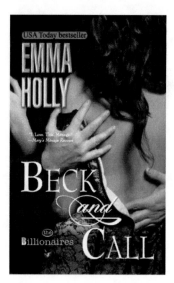

The man everybody wants

Women can't keep their hands off billionaire Damien. The mysterious mogul has it all: fast cars, killer looks, and a brain that just might be his best asset.

Mia loves her job at a PI firm. Her coworker Jake stars in most of her daydreams, so seeing him every day is no hardship.

Jake hasn't believed in human goodness since he worked black ops for the CIA. Romancing innocent Mia is unthinkable, no matter how enticingly submissive she seems to be. Then a case of corporate espionage forces them to pose as dom/sub duo, to catch the eye of accused wrongdoer Damien. No fantasy is off limits for this voyeur—until the attraction the pair exerts lures him to go hands on . . .

"I. love. this. ménage. I am still smiling about these characters. Another outstanding story."—**Mary's Ménage Reviews**

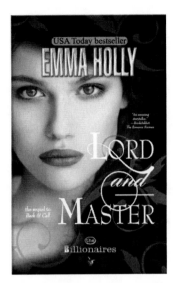

My name is Mia and I'm a lucky girl

Billionaire Damien didn't stop being moody just because Jake and I moved in with him. Fortunately, I've devised a strategy. I inherited a share in an exclusive erotic club, and they're beta testing a role-play game. Surrounded by period perfect detail, members pretend to be Edwardian lords and ladies . . . or stable masters, if they prefer.

By switching up our dynamic, I'm hoping to smooth the snags in our otherwise fabulous ménage. Neither of my lovers has trouble opening his heart to me, but Damien would benefit from exploring his dominant side, and he and Jake could be easier with each other.

That's my goal anyway. My plan might go up in smoke when Jake and Damien concoct their own scheme for me!

The sequel to *Beck & Call*

"So good it defies description . . . The entire premise of the book was fantastic . . . [L]ives up to and exceeds expectations."—Jean Smith, **x-treme-delusions**

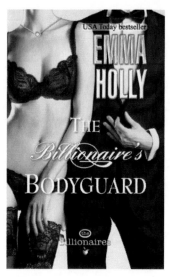

A.J. is as cynical as she is badass, a former cop turned bodyguard. A lifetime of hard knocks taught her not to trust—a handy trait in her line of work. Given the right motivation, she knows anyone will betray their near and dear. Rather than let them betray her, A.J. keeps her shields nailed up.

On the surface, Luke's life seems charmed. He's a Hollywood action hero whose looks inspire fantasies. Known for being easygoing and kind to fans, his latest film made him a billionaire producer. Problem is his high profile is attracting a dangerous class of admirer.

Threats like the one Luke faces aren't new. A.J. saved his life once already. Now he doesn't trust anyone but her to guard him. With a deadly enemy lurking in the shadows, this star-crossed pair better pray A.J.'s skills are sharp!

"A romance story fans of *The Bodyguard* will appreciate . . . a great read and an easy recommend."—Xeranthemum, **Long and Short Reviews**

(formerly published as *Star Crossed*)

Made in United States
North Haven, CT
19 November 2023

44240054R00052